kissed By Flames

Hidden Realms of Silver Lake
Book 3

Vella Day

Can Destiny overcome distrust?

Lily Harper needs protection—a lot of it. Just her rotten luck, some crazy human trafficking Lord wants her for himself. If that doesn't bite the big one, Lily ends up with Birk, a dragon shifter, as her bodyguard. Her last boyfriend was a dragon, and that was a total disaster. That makes Birk definitely off limits. Too bad, because his teal eyes, that glorious body of his, and his tender touch, really light her fire.

The moment Birk sets eyes on the beautiful Lily, his inner dragon starts scratching and clawing to take her as his mate. But holy crap—every time she's near, she pulls away from him, clearly fighting her feelings. She's going to be a real challenge, but as sure as he is a Guardian, he will not let this human's emotions win, especially when it involves his heart.

Chapter One

FATE SURE AS hell was laughing at him today, and Birk Caspian couldn't take it any longer—or rather his dragon couldn't handle not having the delicious Lily Harper in his life. Sure, she was a human, but if he didn't convince his future mate to go out with him—and soon—not only would his inner animal explode, his work would suffer. And that could jeopardize the lives of many people.

Birk extended his claws and then folded his wings as he landed on the lush green grass of the park, just down the street from Lily's apartment. Once he shifted, he straightened his beige button-down shirt and then made sure his hair was out of his face before making his way to her place.

With each step, his nerves increased, which was wrong on so many levels. Being the head of security for SinCas Gems and Metals, he was as tough as they came. So how could some blonde haired beauty with so many emotional walls bring him to his knees with a shake of her head?

Mate, mate, his dragon reminded him.

Like I could ever forget?

The only problem was that Lily kept refusing to go out with him even after his protection detail guarding her had ended, and now it was causing him undo mental stress. It wasn't as if Birk was a weak man—far from it. He was one of the most respected of all the Guardians, even battling some of Tarradon's biggest foes. Yet here he was—feeling dejected and desperate.

Lily will give in this time. I can feel it in my bones, his dragon said, though it sounded like fake encouragement. *And remember to smile for goddess' sake. You look like an ogre most of the time with all your flexing muscles and perpetual frown.*

Fuck off. I got this.

Or so he hoped. He didn't need to explain to his dragon that his constant frown was because of Lily's negative attitude toward dragon shifters in general. His sour disposition also stemmed from the fact that she didn't want to go out with him—now or ever.

He entered her building and strode up to the new wooden door he'd had replaced after her attack. Birk straightened his shoulders and knocked. The addition of the peephole was his suggestion, since the last thing she needed was her ex-boyfriend, Nelor Dobbins—the dragon shifter who'd burned her—to return.

Birk had paid for the door repair, not to earn her favor, but in the hopes it would help her understand that not all dragons were bad. From her reaction to him over the last few weeks though, she might never change her mind.

A china cup hit its saucer and tinkled lightly. Then the voices on the television lowered, but no footsteps neared.

He knocked again. "It's Birk, Lily. I need to talk to you."

As if she could float without making any noise, the knob twisted, and her face appeared around the edge of the door. Instantly, his nails lengthened, and his skin started to harden into scales.

Down, boy.

She's so lovely, his dragon shot back.

Devoid of makeup, Lily was the most beautiful woman he'd ever seen. Her creamy white skin and long blonde hair were in stark contrast to her gorgeous green eyes. And those naturally red lips were made for kissing. When her sweet lavender scent wafted toward him, his dragon clawed his insides.

Birk yearned to run his hand down her arm, but he didn't want to upset her.

"Is something wrong, Birk?" she asked, not stepping to the side to let him in.

Yes, a hell of a lot was wrong, but he'd keep that to himself. "I just stopped by to see how you were doing. Mind if we talk?"

She glanced behind her. He hoped it was to see if her place looked presentable and not to stall for time. He didn't sense she had company.

"Sure," she said, breaking eye contact.

When he stepped past her, heat swelled inside him. If he weren't careful, his dragon would do more than pant and growl when he was near her. She only came up to his chest, and he swore she was even smaller than the last time he'd come knocking, which made him want to protect her even more.

Birk faced her. "Nelor hasn't shown up again, has he?"

She jerked at that dragon shifter's name. "No. He won't come around either, not with a warrant out for his arrest."

Birk's job as head of security at the mines meant he believed in following the rules. Hopefully, Lily appreciated that fact. But unless her brother told her about Birk being a member of the Guardians, she would have no idea how much he cared about people. "No other strange men lurking about?"

When she furrowed her brows, he wanted to take back his question. He sucked at small talk, possibly because most of the women of Tarradon asked him out, not the other way around. Clearly being face-to-face with his mate caused his social skills to disappear.

"No. Once Landry Madison was caught and killed, no one else has threatened me. I'm invisible once more, just the way I like it." She tossed him a quick smile, but it didn't seem to hold much joy— only nervousness.

As much as Birk wanted to reach out and caress her face to soothe her sorrow, he didn't dare. "You're hardly invisible, Lily. You are not only beautiful, but you have an important job. People know who you are."

She broke eye contact once more. "Thank you."

Birk cleared his throat. "I came by in part because I wanted to see if you would have dinner with me. Just so you know, I'm going to keep asking until you say yes." He winked, trying to act cool.

A wink? Are you kidding me? his arrogant dragon asked. *I'll be surprised if she doesn't shove you out the door right now.*

Lily let out a breath. When she touched his arm, heat swamped him once more, and no doubt his ruby scales were doing a dance under his skin.

Sheesh, Lily didn't need to see his brown eyes turn turquoise with lust, or his scales flash under his skin, showing how much she affected him. She was already skittish enough as it was.

"I appreciate the offer, but like I've told you before, I'm not ready to date anyone."

Those words seared his heart. "Is it because I'm a dragon shifter?" Birk asked, keeping his voice soft and low.

"No." Her glance to the floor implied that was a lie.

"Does it bother you that your brother is mated to a dragon?" And that Kyle was now one too?

Her lips twisted. "Not anymore. Nessa is a great person."

And I'm not?

His dragon growled. *Don't act defensive.*

Fuck off, you fire breathing animal.

"My sister is wonderful, but I'm only asking you to dinner. I promise not to shift or shoot fire at anyone." That was assuming he didn't have to protect some innocent person from harm.

"Birk, please. I know I owe you my life for protecting me all those weeks against my brother's former assistant and his minions, but now I prefer to be by myself."

"I understand." No, he didn't, but Birk had no idea how to counter that response. He'd seen how joyous his sister was after mating, and he firmly believed that Lily could be just as happy if she gave him a chance. Just because she said no this time didn't mean he would give up. "I'll stop by again to make sure you're okay."

Lily tilted her chin upward. "I think it would be best if you didn't."

His gut lurched, but begging wasn't his style—at least not yet. "If that's the way you want it, I won't then. Goodbye and take care,

Lily." Each word sliced off a bit of his heart.

It took all of his self-control to walk out of the door and not punch the wall. She'd rejected him—again. Had it been something he'd said? Birk had taken excellent care of her when those men were after his family and hers, yet he never once put the moves on her—and Fate sure as hell knew how much he wanted to.

Her brother, Kyle, told him Lily had also been emotionally scarred by Nelor, but that didn't make it any easier to accept her ultimatum. She was his mate, and he needed her.

Birk was convinced that with time and a little help from his sister and Lily's brother, she would come around. The question was whether he could last that long.

As soon as Birk reached the front entrance to her building his cell chimed. It was his cousin Declan who never seemed to relax when it came to managing the two mines.

"Hey, what's up?" Birk asked in his most cheerful voice. If he'd answered in a tone that reflected his mood, even his fearless cousin might become afraid.

"Where are you?" he asked.

"I just came from seeing Lily. Why?" Declan was well aware of Birk's need to connect with her.

"Are you free now?"

"Yes."

"Good. I could use your help at the gem mine. There's been an altercation between some of the men."

"What do you need me to do?" The employees who worked the late shift were probably just blowing off steam. Most likely Declan was only calling to check up on him.

"I'd like you to coordinate extra security and send them right over."

That seemed lame. "I'll get right on it."

Instead of running back to the park where he could shift and head to the mine, Birk walked slow enough to give him time to plan his next move. He needed to win Lily over, but that was unlikely to happen any time soon.

Birk didn't think it was his looks that turned her off. Hell, many women had told him he was exceedingly handsome, though he bet they were referring to his body more than to his face. Most likely his large build scared tiny Lily. Shit. It wasn't like he could change that. While he'd never met her ex-boyfriend, it was his understanding that he was a big guy too. Lily had been attracted to that type of man at one time. Then Nelor went ballistic on her. Birk would never treat a woman, or anyone else, with that kind of cruelty—unless he was in battle with an enemy and had to fight to survive. With Lily, Birk had deliberately been passive, fearing she'd reject any man—or shifter— who was too aggressive.

He just needed to keep on being himself, even though it hadn't got him very far yet. Eventually, Birk hoped she would take a chance and see the type of person he was: a caring, giving, loving, and highly protective man.

Lily had been hurt. He understood that, but she had let herself judge everyone by that one experience, and he didn't know how to get even a pinhole of light through the walls she had built up around herself.

If you think you've been yourself, you're wrong. You've been nothing but a sullen, over protective ass. You haven't even tried to learn anything about her.

He didn't need this conversation with his dragon. *I know she works for an insurance company and grew up poor.*

If you know so much about her, tell me her favorite color or her favorite food. What is her best childhood memory? Who is her best friend?

A horn beeped, and Birk jumped back to avoid being hit by a car. While a collision with a vehicle would hurt, it couldn't kill him. "*I would know more about her if she didn't push me away all the time. When she does answer my questions, it's with as few words as possible. Since she keeps saying she wants me to leave her alone, it's kind of hard to learn about her, don't you think?*"

"*I get it, but you have to try harder.*"

"I plan to." Just as soon as he figured out how.

For sure, Birk needed help in the relationship department, but he didn't know whose advice he should seek. His cousin Tory was a people person, but he'd never live through the embarrassment of asking for her help. His sister Greer was class personified, but he didn't know how she could help.

First things first; he needed to get to the mine and do his job. Once Birk arrived at the park, he shifted into his dragon form and took off. The more he thought about it, he wasn't even sure why Declan had called him. His cousin was more than capable of handling a little ruckus.

As if on autopilot, Birk found himself over the mine a few minutes later. Not once during the short flight had he checked his surroundings for unfriendly dragons. Crap, he was losing it, and he blamed Lily for making him lose his concentration—damn, sexy woman. Why couldn't she just go out with him? He was positive he could show her a good time.

Birk did have an ace in the hole. If Nessa and Kyle had a get-together, Birk would be in the same room with her and could hopefully charm her, though that wouldn't show her what he was really like—a warrior, a protector, and a good man. Damn. Maybe he was destined to be alone.

When Birk landed and headed to the Sinclair Gem office, he didn't see any major catastrophe brewing outside. As soon as he stepped into Declan's office, his cousin spun around.

"What took you so long?" His lips were pressed tight. Crap.

Birk shrugged. "I came right away."

"What did you do, fight crime for half an hour first?"

"No." Birk didn't need to justify himself to Declan. Okay, maybe he did. Declan Sinclair was the boss over both the Sinclair and Caspian mines, but he was also his cousin.

"Did you contact your men to help out? Because if you did, no one showed up." Declan moved closer. Usually his cousin was easy going, but something seemed to have set him off today.

"Sorry, I forgot to make the call. I was a little distracted."

Declan stared at him as if he'd lost his mind—and that wouldn't be far from the truth. "You forgot? You never just forget. You are the most dependable person I know." He held up a hand. "But don't worry about the skirmish. My men took care of it." Declan gave him that death stare again and then chuckled. "Actually, I called you here to find out what's really going on with you. In the last few weeks, you've been distant and, quite honestly, unreliable."

Birk had never shirked any responsibility in his life. It was what made him so serious. "Nothing happened." Other than Lily.

"Bullshit."

"Fine. If you must know, when I was protecting Lily Harper, I realized she's my mate." There. He'd spilled it.

Declan smiled. "Well, congratulations. You should be happy, but clearly you aren't. Why?"

It was humiliating to mention his failure. "I can't get her to go out with me."

"Seriously?" His tone almost sounded mocking.

"Lily is afraid of dragons."

"Hmm. What does her dragon shifting brother have to say about that?" Declan raised his eyebrows.

"Lily needs time to deal with what her ex-boyfriend did to her, but my dragon is giving me ulcers. I can't sleep. I can't eat. Hell, I can't even remember to call for help one minute after you tell me there is an incident at the mine. That's not like me."

Declan wrapped an arm around his shoulder. "I know. And that's what worries me, but I'm sure you'll figure it out. I'm just hoping it's sooner rather than later. Here is what I propose: take the next two days off. If anything happens around here that needs your attention, we'll call you."

He'd suffered through too many weekends and none of them helped. "Thanks." *I think.*

Not wanting to talk about his humiliating experience to anyone else, Birk left the building and took flight. Just as he was about to reach his condo, he spotted The Wings Bar below. Even though he had an extremely high metabolism for alcohol, a few drinks would help relax him. If that didn't work, Birk might have to consider escaping to Earth for a fresh start.

Chapter Two

"LILY?" ALEA CROWLEY, her boss at Avonbelle Insurance, stepped in front of Lily's desk.

She looked up and instantly sat up straighter. Lily tried to smile, but her lips refused to cooperate. "Oh, sorry. I guess I was off in my own little world."

Try another realm. She'd been daydreaming about Birk again. Even after a restless weekend, her guilt over her attitude with him still hadn't calmed down.

Alea placed a folder on her desk. "We have another case. A warehouse on the west end of town burned down last night. The fire department was called right away, but by the time they arrived, most of the building and its contents were gone."

Lily's heart broke. She picked up the folder and opened it. Inside were photos of the disaster. "What did the arson investigator say?" A lightning strike was one kind of claim, whereas arson was another. If the owner set the fire himself, he'd get nothing.

"He's still investigating."

Lily caught sight of the premium they'd have to pay if it wasn't the owner's fault. "That must have been one valuable warehouse."

"Yes. All of Thresh Toma's construction supplies were inside. The marble may be salvageable, but not much else. Talk to the arson investigator and see if he's learned anything new."

"Sure." The investigator was Josh Gerrard, an old friend of hers who was a super nice guy and extremely thorough at his job.

"Just so you are aware, Toma had another claim a few years back, and while we paid, I always believed something was fishy about it, so don't be too quick to believe everything he tells you. Go by the facts, and don't let him sweet-talk you into believing him. I'm asking you to take the case because I trust you to do the right thing."

Relief and pride filled her. "Thank you. I won't let you down."

Fires were painful for her to investigate. Almost three years ago, Lily had taken a leave of absence after Nelor had burned her back. That incident had almost cost her the job she loved. It wasn't until Alea spoke to the head of the company that she was assured they'd keep her on during her convalescence.

As soon as Alea left, Lily called Josh.

"Hey, Lily."

She hadn't realized he'd put her number in his phone. They had worked together before, and he'd asked her out a few times, so she supposed it made sense he had her contact in his cell. "Do you have time to meet me to discuss the Toma case?"

Her boss was a big believer in face-to-face discussions.

"Sure. Actually, I'm on my way to lunch. How about meeting me at the Hillside Café?"

It was halfway between her office building and the firehouse. "Sure. I'll see you there."

Lily grabbed her purse and pushed back her chair. Once outside, the clear blue skies helped boost her spirits, and she certainly needed the mood elevator. Ever since Landry Madison, her brother's prior assistant and another dragon shifter, had decided he wanted revenge against his former girlfriend Nessa, now Kyle's mate, Lily's life had gone downhill once more.

Landry had fooled her brother into thinking he wasn't capable of harming anyone. Boy, had they both been wrong. She'd met the assistant many times, and he seemed like a nice guy. Clearly, her ability to judge a person's character needed some work too.

That whole incident with Madison was one of the reasons she didn't want to go out with Birk. Yes, when she needed help the most, Birk had been there for her. Hell, he'd taken her and her brother, Kyle, to the mine's safe house, and then he'd watched over her day and night for weeks. Never once did he act inappropriately. So why did she keep turning him down? Deep down, she believed he was an honorable man.

After many sleepless nights of self-examination, Lily finally had to admit the truth to herself—she was falling for him. Hard. If she continued to be near him for any length of time, she feared she'd be a goner. Hell, she would even admit that her girly parts got up and cheered every time he came near her—even now. A part of her longed for the intimacy, but if she gave in, they'd be naked, and then he'd see her scarred back. Birk's look of horror when he saw her would be too much to bear, so she had to be strong.

At one time, she had thought Nelor was a great guy and look what he'd done. Same with Landry Madison, who appeared to be a decent person. To think the asshole tried to kill her brother and had ordered two men to beat her. Obviously, her *good guy o'meter* was busted. No way would she risk trusting her instincts again. Thank heavens her brother had been able to kill the jerk in a to-the-death fight.

After the short ten-minute walk to the Hillside Café—which wasn't situated anywhere near a hill—she stepped inside and was relieved to see Josh already there. Even though she'd told Birk she liked being by herself, that wasn't entirely true. Sitting home alone was fine but going to a restaurant where everyone might pity her terrified her.

With the insurance folder in hand, she strode up to his street side table and slid into the booth across from him. She liked sitting by the window because she could watch the people go by and make up stories about who they were and what kind of lives they led.

"Hey, Lily. Mind if we order first and then talk business? I'm kind of on a tight schedule today," Josh said.

"Perfect. I know what I want. I order take out from here weekly."

The server stepped over to their table and took their drink orders. "What can you tell me about the Toma case?" Lily asked. "Do you think it was arson?"

"It was definitely arson, since we found evidence of an accelerant, but we have no idea who set the fire."

That eliminated some random dragon shifter walking by and deciding to scorch the place. "I see. That will cost the company a lot."

"Not necessarily. Mr. Toma gave me a list of all of the items that were inside his warehouse. Fire destroys a lot of things, but it doesn't make piles of shingles or bags of cement evaporate."

She leaned forward. "What are you saying?"

"What was on his list didn't match what was inside."

Her mind spun. "Meaning we only should pay for the loss of the building and not for much more—assuming he wasn't responsible for setting the blaze?"

Josh smiled. "Exactly."

She'd need more details in order to inform Mr. Toma why the insurance company wouldn't pay as much as he'd hoped. "Can you tell what wasn't there?"

He sucked in a breath. "Yes. We compared the list Toma gave us to the ash residue." He slipped a piece of paper toward her. "I've circled what I can guarantee had been in there before the fire. You might want to ask him about these other items. I suspect he might change his story once he learns we're onto his little scheme."

"Thank you." For the first time in weeks, Lily was optimistic about life, and Alea would certainly be happy about not having to pay out such a large settlement. Lily wouldn't call Mr. Toma a liar to his face until she gave him the chance to correct his statement.

EVEN AFTER BIRK'S days off, his head was still messed up. Out of options, he had to hope that with time Lily would develop a new perspective.

Needing to keep busy so he wouldn't dwell on the hopelessness of his situation, Birk volunteered to head into town to check on something for Declan. Half way to his destination, Birk stopped in his tracks. Lily was sitting in the Hillside Café with Josh Gerrard. Actually, it was his dragon who had screeched and clawed at him to attract his attention. Only then did Birk see his mate, and his hormones had instantly soared and nearly incapacitated him.

He wished like hell his animal would stop fucking with his body and mind. Birk needed to think clearly and have his reflexes in top shape for when danger neared.

Lily was with the arson inspector, so she probably was working on a case—or at least he hoped that was true. He had heard about Thresh Toma's warehouse fire and suspected she'd been given the case to investigate.

As much as he wanted to approach her and ask if this was a date or work related, Birk had already made a fool of himself too many times. He decided it would be best to see if she went back to the office or did something with Josh—from a place where she wouldn't spot him, of course.

Workwise, Josh was known as one of the best arson investigators in the field. When they'd shared a few beers together, Birk quickly learned Josh was a very private person. He was also a great guy, but few humans knew he was a dragon shifter, which meant Lily might have no idea he was one either.

Lily laughed—something Birk had never seen or heard before—and it sent a bolt of jealousy straight through him. Had he looked in the mirror right then, Birk was positive he would have seen his eyes turn turquoise—and it wouldn't have been from sexual excitement either.

Not wanting Lily to spot him lurking, he ducked into a store across the street. He was close enough to keep an eye out for her but far enough away where she wouldn't notice him.

Less than fifteen minutes later, both she and Josh left the restaurant and headed back toward the fire station. Only when she waved goodbye to the investigator and continued on to her office did Birk breathe a sigh of relief.

He followed at a distance to make sure she entered her building where she'd be safe. Unfortunately, she slipped into her car instead. Damn. If she had caught the Thresh Toma case, Birk definitely needed to watch over her. He'd dealt with that panther shifter a time or two, and the guy couldn't be trusted. Not only did he have a temper, he was a loose cannon.

If she were headed someplace else, he'd let her be. Before Birk rushed to the SinCas building to check out the fire at Toma's place, he stopped at the bank and spoke with the manager about some errant payment for the mine. Once done, he charged over to the SinCas roof and flew to Toma's property located on the outskirts of town. For no other reason than curiosity, Birk wanted to check out the fire. If Lily did show up, he'd be there to make sure nothing happened to her.

Not wanting her to spot him should she arrive, he landed about a mile from Toma's property and then cloaked himself before heading closer to the scene. Once hidden at the edge of Toma's property, Birk shifted into his human form.

Five minutes later, when Lily drove in and parked in front of Toma's construction office a few hundred feet from the burned out warehouse, his gut clenched, and his pulse soared.

Birk wanted to join her when she interviewed the man, but because she was an independent woman, she wouldn't appreciate the interference.

Once Lily stepped inside Toma's office, Birk snuck closer to what was once the warehouse. Even though he wasn't an arson investigator, he studied the rubble. Only when the front door to the office opened did Birk return to his hiding place—close enough to hear the conversation and intervene if things turned dicey but far enough away to keep out of sight.

LILY HAD TO admit she was a little nervous visiting Mr. Toma. People who had lost a home or a business were often irrational, bitter, and angry. If they had been responsible for the destruction, they could be a lot worse.

She wouldn't complain since this was what she'd signed up for when she applied for the job, but telling Mr. Toma he might not receive as much as he thought he deserved was always tricky. Desperate people often didn't think before they acted. So far, Lily had never been attacked like a few of her other colleagues had, but there was always a first time. Fingers crossed.

With her folder in hand, she strode up to his office, which was an isolated building in the middle of about ten acres. Because she'd called ahead, he'd be expecting her and her barrage of questions. As soon as she stepped inside, a man jumped up from behind a desk. He was of medium height, about fifty or so, and had a bit of gray at the temples.

He smiled. "You must be Lily."

"Yes."

He came around his desk and held out his hand. "I'm Thresher Toma, but my friends call me Thresh."

She shook his hand. "Nice to meet you." Not really, but she didn't want to antagonize him if she didn't have to. That would come soon enough.

Shaking his head, he gave her the once over and smiled. "I have to say, I didn't expect an insurance agent to be so pretty."

Normally, she would have been flattered, but with the way he was eyeing her, it came out a bit creepy. It was almost as if he believed he could sweet-talk her into writing up the insurance claim in his favor—just like Alea claimed might happen.

Lily might only be thirty-two, but she'd met his type before. The laugh was on him. She was extremely stingy with Avonbelle Insurance Company's money, meaning she'd cut him no slack—unless he deserved it.

"Thank you. I'd like to see the warehouse first before we talk about your claim."

"Why, of course." Outside, on the side of his office, sat an electric cart. "We'll take this. With all the water from the fire trucks, the area is a bit muddy. Don't want your pretty little shoes to get dirty now do we?"

Seriously? Lily couldn't even answer the man's obvious attempt to manipulate her. She slipped in next to him, and because the ruts were rather extreme, she held on tight. The area behind his office was devoid of trees and now lacked one warehouse. She decided not to ask her questions until he stopped the cart.

Toma drove close to the burned out shell of a building. "Bad, huh?" he asked.

"It's a shame." She meant it. Lily stepped out, and her foot immediately sunk into the mud. Ugh. What was wrong with her? She'd completely forgotten to put on the boots she kept in her car for this very purpose. It was all Birk's fault. Or at least, it was her confusion about him that caused her to forget.

She pulled out the folder that Josh had given her. "Can you tell me what was in the warehouse at the time of the fire?"

"I gave the fire inspector a list."

"Do you always keep such detailed inventory?" *Or were you expecting the building to burn?*

He glanced down to the side. "I had purchased items for a new construction job, including some expensive equipment, so I had all of the receipts in my office."

She'd definitely check it out. "I see, and where is this new site?"

He spun to face her. "What difference does it make?"

She smiled sweetly at him—or as sweetly as she could muster. "All the difference in the world."

"Is that how it's going to be? Fine." His flirtatious attitude evaporated. "It's a condominium over on DeKart and Trensor Street, if you must know. I can show you a copy of the invoices."

"That would be helpful in assessing the loss. The arson report says the fire started around ten p.m. Is that right?"

"I think so. I wasn't here."

"Where were you?"

Mr. Toma puffed out his chest. "At the Hog's Head Bar. I have plenty of witnesses to prove it too."

She made a note in her tablet. "Given the presence of an accelerant, arson is suspected. Do you have any idea who might want to do this?"

While it wasn't her job, per se, to find this person, her company needed to know if he'd paid someone to torch his place or if this was some vendetta.

"Fuck yeah, I do—my ex-wife."

Chapter Three

LILY HADN'T EXPECTED that answer. "Why would your ex-wife want to destroy your property?"

Mr. Toma's lip curled. "I'm guessing it's because I'm not always on time with my alimony payments. How the hell do I know what's going through her bat shit crazy head?"

"Burning down your warehouse might cause you to become even more delinquent in your payments."

"Yeah, well Marla is a vindictive bitch—and a not very bright one to boot."

Lily made a note to speak with the wife. "Your daughter, Anita, called in the fire. I'm guessing she was at your house at the time?" His home sat less than fifty feet to the west of his office. If any of the windows had been open, she would have smelled the smoke.

"Yeah. Anita and my two-year old granddaughter, Monique, moved in with me last month when Anita's no-good husband landed in jail. She said she was watching television when she smelled something burning."

Maybe he wasn't as rotten as she first thought. "After she called the fire department, did she notify you at the bar?"

"She texted me, but my eyesight was a little blurry at the time. I had to call a cab just to get home, and by the time I arrived, the warehouse was gone."

"I'm sorry. Where is Anita now?"

"She works at that titty bar on Derlorn Avenue. She's a stripper. My daughter wants to go back to school so she can raise her kid right. She says the pay's good over there."

Lily didn't want to know what she did with her child while she was at work. Maybe the crazy mom watched her. "Did Anita hear anything before she smelled the fire?"

"If she did, she didn't tell me."

He wasn't being cooperative. "I have one more question. It says you had a room full of shingles stored in the warehouse, but the arson investigator said he found no trace of them."

Toma's mouth opened. "Then he's a goddamn liar. Did it ever occur to him that they burned up?"

Lily hated bullies so she didn't answer. Josh had explained that the tar from the shingles would still be there. "Tell me about the Cantoron stone you claimed you had in the warehouse. According to the inspector, the fire didn't burn hot enough to cause it much harm, yet it's not here, just the marble."

He moved closer and glared down on her. "Then whoever set my warehouse on fire must have taken the goods first and used the fire as a cover up."

"That's a nice story, but can you prove it?"

Toma grabbed her arm, and the pain had her letting out a gasp. She struggled, but Toma kept his hold and shook her. "I didn't take pictures of it, if that's what you're asking."

"Get your god damn hands off her now, asshole," came a booming voice behind her.

Toma released her, but from the way his lips sneered and how heavily he was breathing through his nose, he wasn't happy. Lily wasn't sure whether to be relieved Birk had come to her rescue once more or be pissed that he had followed her there.

Toma moved around Lily and tried to get into Birk's face, but she knew him well enough to know he wouldn't be intimidated by the likes of Toma. Not only did Birk outweigh him by a good fifty pounds, he was a half a foot taller.

"Fuck off, Caspian. What the hell are you doing here anyway?"

"I was in the neighborhood and spotted the warehouse—or rather the lack of warehouse. I thought I'd check it out."

"I want both of you to leave." Toma glared at Lily. "I'm calling the insurance company and asking for a new rep—one who knows how to do her damn job properly."

That would never happen. Alea wouldn't kiss his ass.

Before she could wish him good luck with his request, Toma hopped into his cart and took off, leaving her there with Birk. Whoa. She spun to face him and cleared her throat. "Thanks for stepping in, but what are you doing here? Or were you really just out for a spin?"

Birk glanced at the sky. "No. The truth is when I was walking by the café in town, I spotted you through the window with Josh. I'd heard about the warehouse fire and feared you might be asked to investigate."

That might have been true, but it didn't explain his presence. "And you came here to protect me?"

"I won't lie. I wanted to make sure you stayed safe. Toma is not a nice man, as you've now witnessed."

Lily might have told him that she was capable of taking care of herself, but given what just happened even she didn't believe it. "I could have promised to request our company compensate him fully, and he would have let go. It's happened to me before." Just not with someone as creepy as Toma.

As much as Lily wanted to storm off, Birk ignited a deep passion inside her, but it was one she could never act on.

Birk blew out a breath. "The man is dangerous. There's a reason his wife left him."

Lily didn't want to sound ungrateful. Birk had good reason to follow her, but did he worry about everyone? "Then thank you."

"I'll walk you back to your car."

When he placed a hand on her back, a shot of warmth tingled up her spine. While it would have been wise to step away, Lily enjoyed his touch, perhaps a little too much, and let him guide her.

Halfway back to her car, she looked over at him, only to find his gaze on her, making her uncomfortable. "Just so you know," she said, "I plan on working this case. If I have to speak to Toma again,

I'll ask someone to come with me."

"Good."

She had half expected Birk to volunteer for the job, and when he didn't, a small part of her was disappointed.

When they reached her vehicle, he opened the door. "Watch your back, Lily," he said.

Way to scare her. "I will."

Birk didn't move, so she started her engine, backed up, and left. Guilt blasted her once more. Maybe she should have offered to drive him back. Yes, he could fly, but he'd taken time out of his day to watch over her, and she'd barely thanked him. But if she had offered him the ride, during the ten-minute trip, he'd for sure ask her out again, and she wasn't sure she had the emotional strength to turn him down.

With shaky legs and less than a firm grip on the wheel, Lily headed to the office to regroup. If Toma's daughter had been home at the time of the blaze, she might have heard something, especially if someone had snuck into a warehouse and stolen half its contents. Even setting a building on fire had to have been noisy. Though, if Anita was really watching a movie with her daughter, they might have had the volume on high.

Lily pulled into the parking lot of her workplace and sat there, debating her next move. Once they proved Toma had nothing to do with the destruction, there was no reason why Thresh Toma shouldn't receive the value of the warehouse and some of its contents. The first step in getting to the bottom of this case was to make certain Toma had been at the Hog's Head bar when the fire started. Even if he had been there, it wouldn't prove he hadn't hired someone to torch his warehouse.

She'd investigated a ton of false insurance claims before, but this one seemed to be extra difficult.

BIRK HADN'T WANTED to interfere in Lily's case, but the moment that ass touched her, his dragon had gone ballistic. When he stormed out from the forest and shouted at Toma, Birk had been unable to get a read on Lily's expression, other than she was surprised he was there. He supposed he should be happy she hadn't punched him—and had thanked him instead.

Right now, Birk needed to figure out who'd burned down Toma's warehouse. If someone thought Lily knew who'd done it, she might be in danger, and Birk couldn't let that happen. Or was he making a big case out of nothing? It didn't matter. He couldn't change who he was.

The person with the most knowledge about the case was fellow dragon shifter, Josh Gerrard. If his friend was out on another case and couldn't be reached, Birk would leave a message for Josh to contact him.

Sure, he was going behind Lily's back in speaking with the arson investigator, but it was for her own good. When it came to his mate, there was no line he wouldn't cross.

A few minutes after he shifted and took off, he arrived back in town and headed over to the fire station to see if he could catch Josh in person. Luck was on his side. He was in his office, and Birk knocked.

"Come in." When he stepped in, Birk was met with a broad smile. "Caspian. Haven't seen you in a while. What can I do for you?" They shook hands.

Birk wanted to set things straight with Josh from the start. "This is a bit delicate so I'd appreciate your discretion."

"You got it. What does this involve?" He motioned Birk to take a seat.

"Lily Harper. She's my mate."

"Congratulations. She's a great girl."

Because Josh's smile was genuine, his dragon calmed down. "As you know, she's been in a lot of danger recently, what with the whole Landry Madison incident."

"I'm sorry she was caught in the middle. I'm glad everyone is okay now."

Birk nodded. "Today, when Lily went to investigate Thresh Toma's warehouse fire, he became agitated when she more or less accused him of falsifying the report. He grabbed her, and I had to interfere."

Josh's eyes turned turquoise with rage. "Fuck. I should have gone with her. Is she okay?"

"Yes, but I'm worried if Toma is guilty, he might want some kind of revenge."

"How can I help?"

"What can you tell me about the case?" Birk asked.

Josh blew out a breath. "I didn't tell Lily how I knew what wasn't in the warehouse at the time of the fire, but my dragon abilities allow me to sift through ashes and tell what was burned or what wasn't. Trust me when I say that what Toma said was in his warehouse wasn't really there."

"Ah, I see. When Lily told him there was no evidence of the stack of shingles Toma claimed was there, it really pissed him off."

"I'm not surprised, but he should know that the shingles would leave a tar residue after it burned, which was how I know they weren't there in the first place."

"Interesting. Lily promised me that if she had to speak with Toma again she'd take someone with her, but that might not be enough protection against a panther shifter—assuming he's guilty." Birk leaned forward. "Was the fire arson? Or could a dragon shifter have burned down the warehouse—which technically would still be arson?"

"An accelerant was definitely used, but dragons have access to that stuff too."

Bottom line was that Toma might have been involved in all of this mess. "I appreciate the information. If I learn anything more, I'll let you know." Birk stood.

"I won't mention your visit to anyone. When I clear this case up, we should grab a beer sometime. It's been a while."

Josh was a stand-up guy. "I appreciate that, and that's a definite on the beer. It has been too long," Birk said.

He left the fire station and walked up the street to Kyle's office.

As much as he wanted to shadow Lily's every move, it would put her more on edge if she caught him. However, he couldn't leave her to do whatever she saw fit. Lily was a highly motivated insurance agent and would put her job above her safety. The only way to ensure no harm came to her was to ask one of the other Guardians to watch her, and the best candidate was their newest recruit—Lily's brother, Kyle.

Since the Mining Inspector's office was only two streets away, now was as good a time as ever to tell Kyle about being his sister's mate. Birk would then ask for his help in keeping an eye on her.

When he entered the office, Birk asked the woman at the desk if he could speak with him. As soon as he told her his name, she beamed. "You're Nessa's brother."

"I am."

She placed her hand over a glowing light. "Birk is here to see you."

A moment later, Kyle's door opened. "This is a surprise. Come on in." He quickly sobered. "Nessa's okay, isn't she?"

Birk chuckled. "Since you are mates now, you'd be the first to feel if something wasn't right."

He swore Kyle blushed. "I keep forgetting. Have a seat." He stilled. "Oh, no. You're here about Lily, aren't you?"

Birk nodded and sat down. "She's been assigned a dangerous case, and I'm worried about her." Before he told Kyle he was Lily's mate, he explained about the fire and how Toma had grabbed her.

Kyle hissed. "That's terrible. I'll speak with her to make sure she has someone with her if she interviews him again."

Birk held up his hand. "No. She'll know I spoke with you. Don't tell her I came to see you, okay?"

"Why not?"

"Because Lily thinks I'm stalking her."

Kyle raised both brows. "Are you?"

"I guess I am, but it's because Lily is…my mate."

Kyle then pumped a fist. "Yes! Nessa and Greer suspected as much, but they said nothing because they were waiting for you to admit it."

He couldn't believe his sisters never said anything. "I didn't because I didn't want them to tell me it was a lost cause."

Kyle sighed. "I hope it's not. Lily has no idea, does she?"

"No. Cripes, I can't even get her to go out for dinner with me. She just shuts me out completely. I understand why she wants nothing to do with dragon shifters, but I was hoping that with you and Nessa mating, she would come around. Unless, it's just me who's the problem?"

"She's never said anything to me about it being personal. Lily has been through a lot and has become very cynical. My advice is not to give up; she will come around. If anyone can get through to her heart, I believe you as her mate can."

Birk blew out a breath. "Yeah, well, siblings usually don't discuss their feeling about the opposite sex freely—at least in my family we don't. I'm not giving up, but I have to admit constant rejection sucks, man."

"Lily and I are the same in that respect. Don't look at it as rejection; look at it as a *learning curve*." Kyle gave a short laugh. "Things will work out. Give her some time. Tell me more about this Toma fellow."

Birk filled him in on what he knew, including the information from Josh. "If Lily continues to investigate, I fear she might upset someone. As much as I would like to be by her side, or watch from above, she won't be happy if I show my face too often."

"I see, so do you want me to watch her?" Kyle asked.

He was glad Kyle understood. "As much as you can. Lily won't question seeing you around like she would if it were me. I figure she might tell you what her plans are too. In the meantime, I want to investigate Toma, and I can't have Lily around when I do that."

"Of late, it's been quiet in the mining world, but that could change at any moment. Right now, though I have some free time."

Birk smiled. Fate certainly had picked a fine man for his sister.

Chapter Four

DETERMINED TO GET to the bottom of the Toma case, Birk returned to the mine. When he walked into Declan's office, his cousin was on the phone and waved for him to take a seat.

Declan snatched a pen off his desk and then scoured through the drawer until he located a piece of paper. "What are their names?" he asked the person on the other end of the line. He then scribbled something down. "How long have they been missing? Hmm. I can sniff around, but I'm not sure where to start. Any clue how they were taken or where? I see." Declan tapped the pen on the desk while he listened. "I'll get back to you if I find anything. Thanks, Anderson."

Anderson was a Sinclair cousin, another dragon shifter, who worked at the Avonbelle Province Police Department.

"What did he want?" Birk asked as soon as Declan hung up. He wanted something to take his mind off the Toma case.

Declan shook his head. "You won't like it since it involves human trafficking."

His gut churned, and his scales hardened. It was one of the more horrific crimes to him—next to murder. "Tell me."

"Two of Thresh Toma's three daughters are missing."

Toma again? Fuck. "Do you think he did something to them?"

Declan raised one eyebrow. "I know nothing other than the eldest daughter's husband said she's been missing for almost two days now, and he rightfully wants answers. Anderson and his team are stumped, so he called me."

That wasn't unusual. It was often how they got their cases. "And the second daughter?"

"The youngest one, Claire, works at Mercy Hospital as a nurse. When she missed her shift, her supervisor drove over to her house, but all was dark. Worried, she called the missing persons' department. That also was two days ago."

"What about his third daughter? The one who lives with Toma?"

"Anita. Anderson said she's okay."

Birk's mind raced. "What are we dealing with here? Murder or kidnapping?"

"Your guess is as good as mine."

"I don't know if you've had any dealing with him, but Toma is a scum. Did you hear that his warehouse burned down?"

"No," Declan said, sitting up straighter.

Birk filled him in on what he'd learned. "If he burned down his warehouse to collect from the insurance company, there's no telling what else he'd do. While we have no evidence that he committed a crime, Josh Gerrard thinks Toma's claim is at least partially false."

"Why did you speak with Josh Gerrard?" Declan quirked a brow, though he probably could guess.

"Lily is the insurance investigator on the case." He told him about the small altercation she had with Toma.

"I can see why you're interested, but we don't know he's guilty."

"No, but he could be," Birk shot back. "Remember six months ago when Will Session's daughter went missing?"

Declan nodded. "She was about to be sold into slavery by the syndicate when we intercepted the transport. What about it?"

"While we never caught the kingpin, I have no doubt that kind of stuff is still happening in our province. Toma might be involved somehow."

"Shit."

"If Toma did set his warehouse on fire for the insurance money, it's possible he sold his daughters too," Birk said.

His cousin's jaw tensed, and Declan stabbed a hand through his hair. "I'll ask Logan to do an in depth financial analysis on him."

"Call him now. I'll give him the low down."

Declan dialed Birk's brother and put him on speaker. Birk then filled him in.

"I'll be sure to dig deep," Logan said. "Seems to me like this guy has some serious money issues."

"It sure appears that way," Birk said.

"I'm friends with Jackor Drapper who's had experience with Toma," Logan said. "He's one of his competitors. Turns out, Toma cheated him."

"What happened exactly?" Declan chimed in.

"Two or three years ago, Jackor and Toma were bidding on the same piece of land, one that was a prime spot to build condos. Toma won the contract, but Jackor found out later that Toma paid someone to change Jackor's bid."

Birk whistled. "So the guy is dirty through and through."

"Apparently. To be fair, I should mention that it happened a month after Toma's wife left him. I heard he deserved the divorce, but apparently it threw him off his game. He started to drink and gamble after that."

Birk knew all too well how much rejection could harm a person's soul. "What happened to the development?"

"Not only did Toma go way over budget, not enough people bought the units. According to Jackor, Toma still owns several units and is bleeding red."

Birk didn't like to see anyone fail, but Toma might be his own worst enemy. "Good info. Let us know what you find out."

Declan disconnected and blew out a breath. "This is worse than I thought. I'm going to set up a meeting with some of the other Guardians. We need to nip this in the bud if Toma is involved in the human trafficking scheme in any way. One of us should follow him to make sure he doesn't try to mess with Lily. If he's that desperate for money, he might try to pressure her to write up a more favorable report."

"I can do that."

"Good."

Birk always enjoyed working on the Guardians' big cases, but this one might be the biggest of them all since Lily was associated with the case. He chatted a bit more with Declan, told him about his discussion with the bank about the missing payment, and then left. Before he did a fly over of Toma's office to check if he was still there, Birk called Kyle.

Nessa's mate answered right away. "You really are worried about my sister, aren't you?" Kyle said with a bit of a chuckle.

"You know I am, and I have reason to be." He told him that two of Toma's daughters were missing.

"Oh, shit. Are you thinking Toma had something to do with it?" All cheer suddenly disappeared.

"Maybe."

"You don't think he'll come after Lily, do you?"

"I don't know what to think. I just wanted you to be aware that Lily's client has trouble on his hands."

"I just hung up with her and so far, she's fine. In fact, she's at her office doing paperwork. Do you want me to tell her about the women's disappearance?"

"Not yet. I know Lily said she wouldn't go alone if she had to speak with Toma again, but I would feel better if we had some eyes on her—at a distance at least."

"Understood. I'll be there just in case," her brother said.

That was all Birk could ask for. "I appreciate it. I plan to tail Toma to see what he's up to. I'll let you know what I find out."

Once he disconnected, Birk took flight. It was time to find out more about Mr. Thresh Toma.

"WHERE ARE YOU with your report?" Alea asked as she peered down at Lily.

She had been working on the paperwork for the last few hours. "I filled out what I could, stating just the facts as you requested. I also added what Josh said about Toma claiming more was inside the warehouse than what was really there. Before I sign off on it though, I want to ask a few more questions. It is possible someone stole Toma's equipment from the warehouse and then burned down the building to cover his tracks."

Alea nodded. "That's a bit of a stretch. With his daughter in the house, I'm pretty sure she would have seen or at least heard them taking the building materials."

"I agree, but it's what Toma thought happened."

"Did he file a police report claiming theft?"

Damn. "I forgot to check. I'll get right on it."

Her boss studied her for a moment then straightened her shoulders. "Is something wrong, Lily? Usually, you are so on top of things."

Birk happened. Actually, being attacked again by Nelor last month and then assaulted by the men who wanted to punish her brother's mate, had turned Lily into someone she barely recognized. "I'm good."

"All right then. Go ask your questions and then finish up the paperwork. The police can take it from there."

"I will. I plan to interview the ex-wife for her perspective on Thresh Toma."

Alea smiled. "That's a good idea. The more we know, the better. If he did start the fire himself, I sure as hell won't pay him a dime."

Lily smiled. She liked her boss. Alea was a no-nonsense woman. As soon as Alea headed back to her office, Lily made the phone call to the A.P.P.—the Avonbelle Province Police. After being routed to several people, she finally spoke to the person who recorded the claims.

"No," the clerk said. "We have a record of a call into emergency services from an Anita Sussex about the fire, but there's been no follow-up claim about any theft on the Toma warehouse."

"Thanks."

This case was looking more suspect by the minute. After shutting down her computer, she stuffed her report into a folder and headed out to find the former Mrs. Toma. Lily could only hope this woman wasn't as crazy as her husband claimed.

AFTER FOLLOWING TOMA for most of the day, Birk had almost begun to believe the guy was on the up and up. Toma spent his time checking on both of his development projects, never sneaking off to some dark alley to do any kind of illegal deed.

Just as Birk was about to head home, Toma made a detour to the Dragon's Tail Casino. While gambling wasn't against the law, it reinforced what Declan had said about Toma going off the deep end when his wife divorced him.

Not wanting his prey to accuse him of stalking, Birk debated waiting outside until Toma finished, but he then decided it would be easy enough to explain his presence at the casino. He too needed to blow off some steam. If they chatted, Birk would offer his sympathy about his two daughters, all the while studying Toma's reaction.

It was show time.

The interior of the casino was rather large with multiple stations ranging from slot machines, horse betting stations, and dealer tables. Given the size, Toma might not notice Birk at all. Once inside, Toma made a beeline to one of the tables.

Wanting to keep an eye on his man, Birk bought a bucket full of change and headed over to the slots and sat down at one near where Toma was plopping down a pile of chips. Birk estimated it to be about five hundred Denlars—not much more than what he spent for a few days of groceries.

Birk wished he had the ability to become invisible in his human form so he could hover over Toma, but even at this distance, Birk could see the man's mouth twitch and his hands shake. If he hadn't seen Toma grab Lily, he might even be sympathetic to the man's emotional state.

Birk slowly played the slots while he kept a visual on Toma. Curses came from his direction, and when Birk looked over at him, Toma was tossing back another drink. He then slammed down his glass, cursed, and strode away from the table, mumbling and clutching his fists, looking like he wanted a fight. Apparently, things hadn't gone his way tonight.

Not that Birk wanted to enable the man's habit, but he didn't mind donating to the cause if he could learn whether Toma had anything to do with his daughters' disappearances.

He stepped up to Toma and held out a wad of Denlars. "I see you're down on your luck," Birk said, pressing the bills into Toma's hand.

The man's eyes widened. "What's this for?"

"Thought you could give it another go. Nothing is worse than a cheating dealer." Birk nodded to the employee. He didn't like to lie, but it seemed to be the best way to draw Toma to his side.

"You know him?" He didn't wait for Birk to answer. "I thought I saw him deal from the bottom of the deck, the motherfucker."

Birk wouldn't confirm or deny it. "Tell you what. If you win, return my money and give me half of your winnings. If you lose again, you don't owe me anything."

"What's the catch?"

Toma had a right to be suspicious. "Actually, I heard about the disappearance of your daughters and figured you could use a pick me up."

It must have been a play of the light because Birk swore the man's eyes watered. Toma stabbed a hand through his messy hair. "You're right. I'm so upset, I can't think straight. I'm on pins and needles waiting for a ransom call. I don't even want to think of the alternative."

Birk hadn't expected that answer. "So you're trying to win enough money to pay a ransom?"

"Yes."

Most of the demands were for hundreds of thousands of Denlars, but he saw no need to mention that. "Do you have any idea who might have taken your girls?"

"No."

From the way his pupils dilated and then broke eye contact, Toma knew exactly who had them, but Birk wasn't under any delusion that Toma would tell him. No, this was about gaining the man's trust on the off chance he'd leave Lily alone. "See if you can win us some money."

To Birk's surprise, Toma seemed to calm down. After a half hour, he managed to earn a few hundred Denlars. After one more hour, his winnings were quite hefty. Toma gathered his chips, changed them back into Denlars, and then stepped over to Birk who was watching from across the aisle. "Here's what you lent me and half of the earnings. I owe you one, and I won't forget what you did."

Birk could only hope that was true. "Try to keep out of trouble, and good luck finding your daughters. Do the police have any clues?" He knew the answer, but he was curious what they'd told him.

"Those idiots have no idea where to look. They said they can't do much without the kidnappers contacting me first. What a crock."

"That's pretty much standard in these types of cases—or so I've heard." Not wanting to further engage with the man, Birk left, hoping Toma did the same.

As soon as Birk crossed the street, he called Kyle who thankfully answered right away. "Hey, I was just about to call you," Kyle said.

"Did something happen?" Birk's heart pounded.

"No. Lily had a busy day and is now safely tucked into bed. What about you?"

Birk released his clenched fist. "I followed Toma who ended up at the casino. He seems genuinely upset about his daughters disappearing, but I think he knows more than he's saying."

"Do you still think Lily is in danger?"

"Probably. Toma will be even more unpredictable, and the man already showed his temper at the drop of a hat with her. If you could watch her for a few more days, I'm hoping something will break."

"No problem," Kyle said. "I'll have to tell you, she is heeding your warning. When she went to interview Toma's ex-wife today, Lily drove around the block a few times before she parked and went inside."

"Was she lost or being cautious?"

Kyle chuckled. "I'm hoping the latter. Next time you see her, you might ask her what she found out. I'd rather she not know I'm involved."

"I will. I need to speak to Declan first to see what he learned. Depending on the outcome, it might be time to tell Lily everything."

Kyle said nothing for a moment. "Everything, as in Toma's daughters are missing or everything as in you are her mate?"

Birk shook his head. "I wish she was ready to hear we're mates. I don't want to rush her."

"I'm sure she will appreciate that, but Lily is a strong girl, despite how she responds to men. You'll figure out when the time is right."

"I sure as hell hope so."

Chapter Five

B IRK HAD BARELY slept last night thinking about this Toma case and how it might affect Lily. Even though he'd talked with many of his fellow Guardians, nobody had heard anything about a kidnapping or the sale of two women in their twenties. Declan and the others planned to expand their search today, but to help things along, Birk had asked a few of his siblings to put out a few feelers around town. He could only hope something panned out soon.

Frustrated at the lack of progress, he headed to the Caspian mines and went straight into the office. Nessa happened to be at her desk. "You're just the person I need to talk to," he said.

His sister was dressed in her usual khaki pants and baggy shirt with the Caspian logo on the pocket. Despite the dirt smudges on her cheek, she looked good. The glow of happiness did wonders for her.

She looked up and frowned. "I'm not a fan of dark circles. You need to sleep more." Birk swallowed a response. "So, tell me what can I do for you today, my troubled brother? And no, I don't know anything more about the missing women."

Damn. Kyle must have told her. "I'm worried about Lily."

"Because she's working on the Toma case? Or because she's your mate and you're just being your usual over-protective self?"

All he could do was shake his head. "Did Kyle tell you we were mates?"

"No. The moment I saw you with Lily after her attack, I could sense the bond forming between you. Let's be honest. Once your bodyguard duty ended, you haven't been yourself. You never used to mope around. Even Declan has commented on it a time or two."

"Can't anyone keep a secret around here?" Birk pulled up a chair in front of her desk and dropped down onto the seat. "I think I'm going crazy."

Nessa smiled. "Ask her out again."

His sister wasn't as smart as he thought. "You don't think I've tried that? She keeps turning me down."

"And why do you suppose that is?" his sister asked, leaning on her elbows and looking way too smug.

Birk stilled. "You know something I don't?"

Nessa chuckled. "You have to ask me that?"

Now he felt like a fool. Women had a second sense about these things. "Sorry."

She smiled. "Look, I know you're upset that Lily hasn't thrown herself at your feet, but I can hazard a guess why she wants little to do with you."

Birk sat up straighter. "Why's that?"

"She likes you too much."

A laugh burst out, but it held no mirth. "You're jerking my chain, and I don't appreciate it."

Nessa tilted her head and sighed. "I'm being serious. What if you two became romantically involved and made love?"

"I'd be the happiest man on earth."

"You might be, but in the process, she'd be naked and you'd see her back."

Birk didn't see the point. "I know that asshole burned her, but it's not like I haven't seen what fire can do to skin before."

"Would you be repulsed?"

His sister was talking crazy. "Fuck no. Lily can't help what happened to her."

Nessa leaned back. "She hasn't come out and told me exactly why she's so skittish, but Kyle said that every man she has been close to has rejected her once they see her scars."

Birk pushed back his chair. "Then I'll tell her I don't care about what her back looks like."

Nessa shook her head. "She won't believe you."

"Why not?"

His sister sighed. "If you are that clueless, I can't help you. What you need to do is to take a break and do some deep thinking. Hopefully some answers will come to you." She snapped her fingers. "And I have just the place."

"I tried taking a weekend off, but it didn't do any good."

"Don't judge until you hear my suggestion."

"I'm not going to some fancy spa or portal down to Earth for a bit. I'm needed here."

She held up a palm. "I have something closer in mind—like an hour away."

Then why didn't he know about it? "Where is this amazing retreat? Believe me, I would do anything to get a new perspective on things."

"Have you ever been to the eternal flame?"

"Maybe fifty years ago."

Nessa studied him. "Do me a favor and check it out. While you are there, be sure to toss a coin in the fountain and make a wish."

Birk didn't even want to know what superstition lay behind that request. "How will going there help me figure out what I can do to earn Lily's trust?"

"When I went there with Kyle, we ran across a wise woman by the name of Fay Forrester."

That name sounded familiar. "The one you said was tiny and had wings?"

"Yes. She could disintegrate—if that's the right word—into hundreds of fireflies and disappear."

He didn't believe in fairies. Most likely Nessa had conjured her up since she'd wanted answers about who was trying to kill her. Maybe he should save himself a trip and talk to the Four Sisters of Fate instead. They were wiser than anyone. The problem was that unless it was a matter of life and death, they were reluctant to give advice or help. "If I go and nothing happens, will you talk to Lily for me; tell her I don't care about her back?"

"When you return, we'll discuss your options."

That was all he could ask for. "I'll see you soon then—hopefully with a plan."

Birk wasn't sure why he agreed to visit some old flame, but Nessa acted as if it would help. Right now, he had to take whatever advice he could get, especially since his sister and Lily seemed to be growing closer.

Once outside, Birk shifted then took off toward the spot where the four provinces of Tarradon met. It was said that the flame was a symbol of the cooperation between the provinces, forged long before he existed. If he recalled correctly, the flame was situated in a dense forest surrounded by an untouchable preserve.

As he flew to the middle of the realm, his mind began to relax, and he was able to enjoy the beauty of Tarradon. The hills were a lush green and the air sweet. He almost believed what Nessa said was true—that Lily didn't hate him. In fact, she might even be attracted to him, but that she feared he'd reject her. That actually made sense. All he had to do was let her know they were mates, and she'd understand that he would never leave her.

Lily was beautiful, and it didn't matter to him if her body wasn't as perfect as she wanted. He loved her just the way she was. In fact, part of Lily's allure came from her having been a burn victim survivor. Birk had been around long enough to know that people who were conditioned to believe they were less than ideal would not take someone's word for it. That meant he'd just have to show her.

By the time he spotted the flame, his spirits had risen. Because of the density of the trees, he landed in an open field two miles from the actual site, shifted, and trekked in on foot. He thought he might run into a tourist or two, but it seemed as if he had the whole forest to himself.

Today, the birds seemed to chirp louder than usual, and the air smelled cleaner. It was said this part of the realm possessed magic, and it just might be true.

When he arrived, no one was there. No fairy. No shaman. Nobody.

Did you expect someone to walk out of the forest and tell you how to win over your mate? his dragon asked.

Of course not. But a guy could hope.

Birk stepped over to the fountain, dug a hand in his pocket for a coin, and then turned his back to the water. Nessa wouldn't believe him if he said he'd made a wish, so he decided to video it for her. With the phone camera in hand he pressed the video button. "Nessa, this is for you. May Lily fall madly in love with me and want to be my mate."

He tossed the coin behind him, and when he heard it splash, he shut off the video.

Clapping came from his right and startled the shit out of him. Birk spun toward the sound and relaxed when he spotted a petite blonde. She looked as if she were trying hard to hold in a laugh. For some reason he felt compelled to explain. "My sister told me that wishes often come true here, so I had to toss in a coin."

The stranger moved closer. "They do come true, if it is meant to be."

"Good to know."

She held out her hand. "I'm Fay Forrester."

Holy shit. "The fairy?" he blurted.

He swore she blushed. "Yes, and I take it you're Nessa's brother?"

Only then did he remember he'd mentioned her name. "I am. Name's Birk Caspian."

They shook hands, and the woman seemed to be all flesh and blood. "Did I hear you had woman problems?"

Now he was the one to have heat race up his face. According to Nessa, Fay had powers, so he had nothing to lose by asking her about his situation. "I do. Lily, who is human, has no idea we're fated to be with each other."

"I see. And she's unwilling to hang out with a big dragon shifter like you, is that it?"

How did she do that? "More or less."

Fay closed her eyes and suddenly transformed into what could best be described as a six-inch tall being with gossamer pink wings. She whipped around him twice before landing on his shoulder. While he could have swatted her away, she must have had a reason for being there. A moment later, she flitted in front of him again and transformed back into a woman.

"Sorry about that," she said, "but I needed a better sense of what was going on. I'm sorry to say that Lily is in danger."

His blood boiled, and the fire in his belly nearly shot out of his hands until he realized she probably had no idea what she was talking about. Then Nessa's words came back to him, and he decided to give her a chance. "From whom?"

"From the men Thresher Toma is dealing with."

His knees almost buckled. How the hell did she know anything about that? Birk opened his mouth to ask her more questions, but the shock of her information had turned him mute for a moment. "Who are these men, and where can I find them?"

"They're working out of Glen Meadow at the moment."

Before Birk could question her further, Fay returned back into her small self and flew away.

"Wait!" He ran after her until she separated into hundreds of fireflies. Birk stopped and stood there for a long time hoping she'd return. When it was clear she wasn't coming back, he left.

For some reason, walking took a lot of effort. Hell, his mind could barely process how to put one foot in front of the other. If Lily's life was at risk, he needed to warn her. Now.

Birk pulled out his phone to tell Kyle to keep an eye on his sister, but he had no cell service. Well, damn. He was tempted to check out Glen Meadow for himself, which was on the outskirts of the province, but he decided it was more important to protect Lily.

While Kyle might not mind watching over his sister for another hour, that job belonged to Birk, whether she wanted him to or not.

Once he made that decision, his legs began to work again, and he sprinted down the trail. When the field appeared into view, he shifted and flew away. This time, he didn't dawdle. Instead, he flew close to the ground, catching the strongest air currents and reaching the roof of the SinCas building in record time. As soon as he shifted back, he called Declan to suggest he focus his attention on Glen Meadow.

"Tell me exactly what you found out," his cousin said.

Whether or not Declan would believe the word of a fairy, it was the best lead they had so far.

"I met a woman—a fairy, if you will—who said that Lily is in danger from the men Toma has been dealing with."

"Did she give you any details? Like whether these men were kidnappers, murderers, or merely worked for Toma?"

"No." Birk was surprised Declan didn't demand to have some proof that a real fairy existed.

"Did this fairy person tell you how she knew this?" Declan asked.

"No, and just as I was about to ask she took off."

"Damn. Did your fairy friend tell you her name?"

Birk couldn't tell if Declan was mocking him or not. "Fay Forester."

"The same woman Nessa and Kyle ran into."

"Yes."

Declan didn't answer for a moment. "What's your next step?"

"I need to tell Lily everything—and by that, I mean what I found out about Toma. I'll also have to tell her that we are mates and that she is in danger."

"I think that's smart."

He debated asking him to question Toma, but he didn't want to tip off the man. "How about you check out Glen Meadow? I'm thinking it's where Toma's daughters are being held hostage—assuming they are still alive."

"Definitely."

The tension in Birk's shoulders released somewhat. "Thank you."

"Don't worry. We'll get these guys."

"That's all I can ask."

Once they disconnected, Birk shifted again. This next conversation might be the hardest in his life—and the most important.

Chapter Six

LILY SHUT DOWN her computer and was about to go home for the night when Cassie, the office receptionist, buzzed her. "Ms. Harper, there's a man here to see you."

Thinking it must be Birk, her heart raced. Stupid body. Her hormones exploded right after the adrenaline rush. Lily was so torn. If she'd never been burned, she would be chasing Birk since he was everything she wanted in a man. The scars covering her entire back convinced her daily that she needed to keep her distance however.

Lily probably should say she was busy, but damn, she would enjoy seeing him, especially after the last few days—her stress level had been sky high. And then there was this whole creepy feeling that someone had been following her. She would have mentioned it to Kyle, but whenever she turned around, no one was there. It certainly hadn't helped that Mr. Toma seemed ready to blow. He'd called several times already to find out the status of his claim. "Send him in."

Lily ran her hands down her hair and smoothed out her shirt. When the door burst open, her heart stopped. She jumped up and nearly toppled her chair. "Mr. Toma!"

He stepped toward her desk and planted his hands on the edge. "I have to know how much I'm going to get from my insurance claim."

"I told you over the phone these things take time." There was no need to mention that the police needed to be certain he wasn't involved.

After she'd spoken with his ex-wife, she could almost believe he'd paid someone to set the fire. However, after learning his two daughters were missing, her sympathy had shifted.

"Why?" His voice rose, and she slowly moved her hand toward the button on the side of her desk to call for help. Customers were often frustrated with the process of claims and some became abusive. They'd installed the silent call for security a year ago when one of their agents was attacked and received a broken nose and a dislocated collarbone. Alea didn't fool around when it came to her staff; they were like family. She told them if for any reason they didn't feel safe with a client, they just needed to push the button before things escalated.

"Actually, I just turned in the report a few minutes ago, so it's out of my hands. It takes time to process such a large sum. You'll get your money as soon as the police tell us we can."

He puffed out his chest. "When they do, how much will I get?"

Crap. She couldn't lie. "I recommended half of what you asked for." She inhaled and held her breath.

He leaned even closer, his eyes focused hard on her face. "You believed that weasel arson investigator who said I lied?" His eyes shifted in every direction, and spittle dripped down his chin. Lily pressed the button.

"Mr. Toma. I suggest you speak with Inspector Gerrard yourself and ask for his results. He has the chemical analysis report that shows what you had and what you did not have in the warehouse." That wasn't totally true, but all she needed was for this man to calm down.

"I told you, I was robbed," he said between gritted teeth.

"Did you file a police report?" His eyes went wide. Gotcha!

"No, but that shouldn't matter." The left side of his lip curled.

Lily held up her palms, trying to stall for time. "Please calm down, Mr. Toma. I imagine the fire, along with the disappearance of your daughters, has you not thinking straight. I'm sure we'll figure something out."

His skin turned white. "What do you know about my daughters?"

"Nothing. I swear. Just that they are missing. I can't imagine the pain you must be going through." Lily didn't usually babble, but she was afraid of Toma.

Just as he moved around the desk toward her, two security guards rushed in. "Sir!" Before Toma could reach her, the guards grabbed him. "Come with us."

Toma glared at her and then sneered. "This isn't over."

Lily's legs weakened, forcing her to sit back down. Over the years, she'd encountered some pretty pissed off people, but none seemed as violent as this man. Part of her wanted to call Birk and ask if he'd escort her home, but the other half decided against it. She was strong—or so she wanted to believe.

After pretending to do a little work at her desk until her breath slowed and her hands stopped shaking, she sucked it up and left the almost-empty office. As Lily walked toward her parked car, she kept a lookout for anyone hiding between vehicles ready to jump out at her.

Once she made it, she slid in and locked her door. Her heart was still racing too fast. She was a mess, all because of Toma. It wasn't just him though. It was everything that had happened in the last few months. Between her ex-boyfriend and the attack on her brother's mate, Lily's nerves were stretched taut.

Even driving the two miles home took all of her concentration. When she finally reached her apartment, she rushed inside the building. When she spotted Birk waiting for her by her front door, she was tempted to hug him.

"Hi," she said a little out of breath.

He smiled. "Hi, yourself." Birk closed the gap between them and then clasped her shoulders. "You're pale. And you're shaking. Are you okay?"

She shook her head. The temptation to press her body against his was strong, so she grabbed just a bit of comfort by clasping his big bulging arms—but only for a moment. "I could be better. Want to come in?"

His grip tightened, and his eyes widened, no doubt trying to figure out why she'd just done a one-eighty on him.

"Of course."

Once she stepped inside her apartment, Lily's anxieties shot up again as conflicting emotions ran through her. Leaning on Birk to draw on his strength would be wonderful but way too easy. She needed to figure things out for herself, and falling for him would end in disaster. Been there done that.

"Can I get you something to drink?" Her voice came out higher than she'd wished.

"I think *you* could use a glass of wine. I'll join you if you have some."

One glass wouldn't hurt, but she needed to keep her wits about her. "That sounds good." Lily ducked into the kitchen only to realize she and Nessa had finished off the last bottle. "I just remembered that I'm out of wine. Is tea okay?" she called out.

"Sure. Whatever you're having is fine with me."

As she fixed the drinks, she debated how much she should tell Birk. Knowing him, he'd rush out and confront Toma, and that would only cause the man to lash out at her in earnest the next time. No, she'd say Toma visited her, but not mention that she'd had to call security. As she dunked the teabag into the hot water, Birk came up behind her. When he placed a hand on her shoulder, she nearly leaped out of her skin.

"Tell me what's wrong."

The sympathy in his voice nearly broke her spirit. Lily hadn't realized until now how much she missed confiding in someone. That person used to be Kyle until he met Nessa. Lily spun around. "Toma came to the office a little while ago."

Birk's eyes changed colors right in front of her. "What did he say? Did he hurt you?"

"No, but he might have if I hadn't called security on him." Damn. She hadn't meant to confess that.

Birk picked up the two cups. "Come sit down and tell me everything."

"I'm fine—physically at least."

Birk set the drinks on the coffee table, guided her to the sofa, and then sat next to her. "I need to know what happened and don't leave anything out."

Lily proceeded to tell him every detail of what went on with Toma at her office. Birk waited until she finished before commenting. "How did you hear about his missing daughters?"

Lily picked up her cup and blew the steam off the surface. "I spoke with his ex-wife."

His hand tightened on his cup. "Why? Did you suspect her of setting the fire?"

She didn't appreciate his sharp tone. "Toma told me he thought his ex-wife might have hired someone to torch the warehouse, and I wanted to hear her side of the story."

His chest caved a little as if he'd let out a big breath. "Did you go alone?"

"Yes. I know, I know, but I only said I wouldn't speak with Mr. Toma by myself."

Birk waved a hand. "You're right. Go on. What did she tell you?"

"Let me say upfront. I liked the woman and actually felt sorry for her for having to put up with that ass for so long. Apparently, when Mrs. Toma met her future husband, he was a really nice guy. The way she told the story, it sounded like they had a good life, one with a future. I think the best thing about the man was that he loved his daughters unconditionally. Then Mrs. Toma became ill, and her husband had to work harder and longer hours to pay for her care. That's when things became strained between them."

"I've seen that happen to many couples. Did Mrs. Toma say what caused her to divorce him?"

"Yes. The downturn in the real estate market hit Toma hard. Apparently, he built some condos that didn't work out as planned, and he lost a lot of his money. That was when he began to gamble.

From there his problems escalated."

Birk sipped his tea and almost looked refined with a china cup in his huge hands. "Do you think Mrs. Toma had anything to do with the burning of the warehouse?"

"No. Was she angry that her ex was often late with his alimony payments? Sure, but she appreciated that he offered their middle daughter and granddaughter a place to live after their son-in-law was arrested for petty theft."

"Did she have a theory about who burned down his warehouse or who might have taken their daughters?"

Lily only liked to talk in facts, but her gut had been working overtime. "Marla Toma said that given the mounting excuses her ex-husband gave her for why he couldn't pay her monthly allotment, she believed he owed money to someone. While she has no proof, she thinks it's possible this loan shark decided to take the one thing he held dear—his family."

Birk's mouth opened, but only for a moment. "That's really helpful. I'll ask around. I know where Toma gambles, and I'm betting someone there must have heard him talk about needing to pay someone off."

Talking about the case with Birk was exciting. She rarely had the chance to discuss anything about her work. "Do you think Toma set the fire to his warehouse so he could pay off this guy?"

Birk shrugged. "It's not my job to know. Right now, my focus is on keeping you safe."

Anyone would love a protective man, but Birk was a bit smothering. "What makes you think I'm in danger anymore?" She held up a hand. "Sure, Toma clearly is in desperate need of cash and probably thinks I suspect him of torching his place, but he's already threatened me. Once he receives his money—or rather if he does—I believe he'll leave me alone."

Birk lifted the cup of tea from her hands and set it down. "There's more to it than that."

Her heart dropped to her stomach. "What is it?"

"I haven't been totally honest with you."

That was the last thing she expected Mr. Straight Arrow to say. "I don't understand."

He twisted in the seat to face her. "I need to tell you about what I did today to give you a little background."

Given the way Birk was having a hard time making eye contact, she probably wasn't going to like what he had to say. "I'm listening."

"I'm sure you'll agree that things between us have been, at best, strained." He exhaled hard and held up a palm. "I get it. No one likes to have some strange man hanging around all the time, pestering her to go out with him."

When he looked at her, she felt obligated to answer. "You're not some strange man, but I'll admit it can get a bit stifling at times. However, I've been around worse."

"Thank you. It's because I have reason to believe you are in serious danger."

She shook her head, mostly because she didn't want to believe it. "I don't think Toma will come around anymore."

"I'm not talking about him."

Okay, now her stomach was clenching and tumbling. She wished Birk would be more specific. "Does Kyle know anything about this complication?"

"Not yet. Let me start by saying that we are—oh fuck—maybe I should begin with the first time I met you."

She'd never seen Birk come unraveled like this. "You can tell me anything."

He nodded. "The first time I saw you lying on the floor, something came over me—a wave of protective need—and I felt this instant connection. I didn't want anyone else touching or coming near you. It was like a piece of my soul was attached to you…Ugh, I suck at this kind of stuff, and I am screwing up trying to explain it to you." His lips pressed together as if he was waiting for her to say she felt the same thing.

Birk's words touched her more than she could say. "I remember very little about those first few hours after the attack. I was still in shock when I came to, and it wasn't until after you took me and Kyle to that safe house underground, that I became aware of what you were. Even then, I had no idea why Nessa was hanging around Kyle. Now I know it was because they were mates." Birk's eyes changed from a rich brown to that beautiful teal color. Then like a tsunami, it hit her. "Are you saying that I'm your mate?"

He finally let out a breath. "Yes, but that doesn't mean you have to accept me. I know I can be over protective and a bit uncouth—or so Nessa tells me—but I'm willing to wait until you're ready."

Lily had no words. She was Birk's mate? For real? Birk was, after all, a dragon shifter, and the last dragon shifter had hurt her badly.

Her heart fluttered as excitement filled her, but at the same time, dread pooled in her stomach. Lily wanted to believe that Birk was different, but she was afraid to take the leap. Her insecurities about what he would do when he saw her back were strong.

Could she take the chance that he wouldn't be disgusted and run? That was the gold winning question right there.

Then again, Kyle had never been so happy as when he'd mated with Nessa, and then again when he was transformed into a dragon...Oh, no. "Are you saying that if we mated, I'd have to be a dragon too?"

His smile wobbled. "I don't know any way to stop it, but Kyle likes being one."

That was a deal breaker. Lily sat up straighter. "Kyle is a born fighter. I'm not."

"Just think if you could shift into a dragon, you could shoot fire at Toma if you wished—or Nelor!"

She could never hurt anyone—well, maybe Nelor. "I barely know you."

When the muscles in his face sagged and the light in his eyes dimmed, she wanted to take back every word.

"That's why people date," he said. "Look, I'm not asking you to strip naked and make love with me this minute. I mean...I'd like that, but I like you as a person and want you to get to know me too."

Did he really like her? Or was that his hormones talking? She was so confused.

Lily finally admitted that this indecision was driving her crazy. Bottom line was that she had to finally pull up her big girl panties and just show him that she cared. She could no longer deny that she was falling for Birk, big time. No more hiding!

In order for them to move forward though, or for her to accept a rejection and move on, she needed to see his reaction first hand—in the light of day and not in the throes of passion. With her heart slamming against her ribs, Lily took a deep breath, turned away from Birk, and grabbed the hem of her shirt. Tears brimmed on her lashes as she raised the material over her head, waiting for the intake of breath or the grunt of disgust.

Chapter Seven

BIRK INHALED, NOT because of what Lily's back looked like but because of what she had been through. The strength and bravery it took for her to remove her shirt, showed the amount of trust she was giving to him. This woman touched his heart and soul like no other ever could.

"You're beautiful," he whispered. Birk expected her to turn around, but Lily just sat there.

Then Nessa's words came back to him about how Lily was sensitive about her burned back. Is that what this was? Some kind of warped show and tell? Sure, the skin was dimpled and twisted, but the coloring appeared more or less normal. From the way her shoulders were moving and the little sounds she was making, he realized she was crying.

Birk placed a gentle hand on her shoulder. "Lily? Look at me, please."

She grabbed her shirt from her lap and slipped it back on. The tears streaming down her face were cutting slices in his heart. Without thinking, he scooted closer and gathered her into his arms. For once, she didn't struggle. In fact, Lily buried her head against his chest and seemed to let out all the emotion she had been bottling up inside.

Birk pressed his face against her hair and inhaled her delicious scent—fresh like the forest and as pure as the air high above the realm. He gently rubbed her back and spoke soft words of encouragement to her. When Lily finally calmed down, she looked up at him and leaned back. "Well?" she asked.

"I know you were burned, but it doesn't bother me if that's what is worrying you. Lily, I know you can't really understand this, but we are fated to be together. To me, you are beautiful both inside and out. A little scarring doesn't matter to me." He took off his shirt. While his dragon healed his wounds, there was one ugly gash near his shoulder that was a bit lumpy. He picked up her hand and ran it over the five-inch slice. "Does this offend you?"

She lightly ran her finger over the gash and then slipped her hand from of his grasp. "No. Why would it? Scars on men are sexy."

He chuckled. "Then why would your scar bother me?"

She looked off to the side. "I guess because it has offended every other man who has seen it."

Birk tried hard not to let his jealousy show. "Since no other man will ever have the chance to look at your lovely body again, you'll never have to worry about someone else's ridicule. What you need to understand is that you are extremely important to me—more important than life itself. If I mess this up, it'll kill me."

She smiled briefly, and his whole insides rejoiced, swamping him with hope and joy. It was when she placed her palm on his chest that his dragon cheered.

"I'm not good at expressing myself either. To be honest, I've kept my distance because I feared if you saw my back you'd run away."

He lifted her hand and pressed her fingers to his lips. "Never."

Lily slipped her hand out of his once more, clearly not ready for what he wanted.

Birk ran a finger down her cheek. "Tell me what you're thinking. Are you terrified of us being mates? Slightly happy about it? Or cautiously optimistic?"

Lily hiccupped and then smiled, her lips wobbling. "I think cautiously happy. Yes. Cautiously happy. That's it, and hopeful. I would give anything to erase my past and my prejudices, but if anyone can change my mind about what happened, it's you."

Those words were more than he could have hoped for. "I'll take it. One step at a time it is. Just tell me if I move too fast or if I scare you."

Lily placed a hand on his cheek, and Birk swore his skin burned from her wonderful touch. "I trust you."

Yes! Birk wanted to grab her, hold her close, and then kiss her silly, but he wouldn't. At least not right now. "Now that the air is cleared about how I feel about you, I need to warn you."

She stiffened, and he wished he'd not told her so soon. "Warn me about what? And don't say Thresh Toma wants to kill me."

"No. Not him. At least I don't think so." He told her about flying to the eternal flame and meeting a woman who he could only describe as some kind of fortuneteller. "I'd been told she is very wise and quite magical."

"I've heard of the eternal flame. Kyle mentioned something about Nessa talking to a woman there."

"Yes. This woman, Fay Forrester, remembered Nessa and then told me someone affiliated with Thresh Toma would harm you. I had to take her seriously." He held up a hand. "Before you ask, I never mentioned his name to the woman. She just knew."

"Are you saying Toma hired someone?"

"I don't know what to think. Fay just said you were in danger from some of Toma's associates. That's all. She said these men were based out of Glen Meadow. Have you ever been there?"

She glanced off to the side. "No. Never. Even if I believed this woman, why would someone I've never met want to harm me? I've already turned in my report about the arson case. There is nothing more I can do to help or harm Mr. Toma."

Lily was right. Maybe he was overreacting, but he couldn't help it. "Maybe these men from Glen Meadow are the ones who took Toma's daughters."

She pressed her lips together. "Suppose that's true. That's no reason to target me. I don't work for him. If they hated you, for example, then yes, hurting me could serve their purpose."

"You're right, but I can't ignore what this woman told me. For now, I'm not leaving your side."

Her eyes widened, and her face reddened. "I know we are mates, but didn't you tell me that I have a say in this?"

"No." From the way Lily's lips had firmed, he might be in for a battle. Shit. Birk was so used to getting his own way that he didn't stop to think that his feisty woman might rebel. "I mean, yes, you do have a choice. I'm sorry, but I could never live with myself if anything happened to you. I won't be by your side every moment of every day like I was before, but I will be watching you—even if it means sleeping in your hallway."

She grabbed his arm and squeezed. "Birk. Don't do this. Please. Can you give me some evidence that I'm really in danger?"

"Declan, Thane, and Finn are at Glen Meadow right now, trying to find out that answer, but if this oracle does have psychic abilities, she might be talking about the future."

Lily slumped back against the sofa. "Fine. You can stay here, but I'm going to work and will go about my business as usual."

He let out a big breath. "Thank you. And no problem with you doing your job." It was the best he could ask for. Needing some help, Birk pulled out his phone and called Kyle.

"Is Lily okay?" her brother asked without saying hello.

"Yes. I wanted to update you on something. I've told her every-thing, but I need one last favor."

"Anything."

"I need to run an errand right now. Can you make sure she's safe while I'm gone?" Birk asked.

"Sure. I can be there in a few minutes."

"I'll wait for you outside."

She grabbed his arm. "You really believe something is going to happen, don't you?"

"I hope I'm wrong, but I won't take any chances."

"I get it. I do." Lily moved closer, leaned forward, and brushed her lips against his cheek. "Thank you."

Hormones drenched his body, and his mouth didn't work for a

moment. "You're welcome. I know that my hovering can be a bit claustrophobic, so I'm going to see if I can find another kind of help—one that won't smother you as much."

She furrowed her brows. "By asking Kyle to stand watch?"

"Yes, but I can also ask some of my brother's, or even Nessa, to take a few shifts."

"Okay. I understand."

He was thrilled that she didn't balk. Birk stood. "I'm going to wait outside for Kyle, but I shouldn't be gone too long."

"Where are you going?"

"I'll tell you when I return."

Lily rose and when she gave him a brief hug, much of the tension of the last few weeks disappeared. "Thank you again," she said.

He was about to say it was in his nature to protect her, but that might diminish her appreciation. "You're welcome."

You need so much work on being romantic, his dragon said.

Fuck off. I'll figure it out.

You better.

Birk waited outside for Kyle, and when he arrived, he gave him a more detailed rundown of what he'd learned. "I want to ask the Four Sisters a favor, and I hope they can help me."

"Good luck."

Knowing Lily would be safe, Birk rushed to the park near her apartment, shifted, and headed to the edge of town toward the Four Sisters Pottery store. He wasn't going to ask them to divulge the names of the men Thresh Toma was tangled up with, since they wouldn't tell him anyway. He hoped they could help in another way.

It was just past closing when he arrived, but the light in the back was on, so he rapped on the front door. When Acacia and Poppy came out of the back together, the store lights lit up.

They both answered. "Birk, it's always nice to get a visit from a Guardian. Come in," Poppy said.

Only a rare few—the four sisters being ones—knew who the Guardians were. "I've come to ask for a favor." As always.

Poppy smiled. "How can we help?"

Birk explained about how his mate was in danger, though he said he didn't really know the details. "There is a huge gem and metal conference coming up in a few days, and most of the Guardians will be in attendance, which means we're going to be shorthanded. It's possible I'll have to take care of something dire. Is there anything I can do, before mating with her, which would allow me to sense if she is in danger in case I can't be with her?"

The two women looked at each other. Then Acacia reached out and ran her hand above his heart where his scar existed. "Perhaps. Can you give us a scale from right here?"

"I can do that." He'd learned not to question their methods. "I'll step outside. If I shift in here, I'll destroy not only every pot and plate but part of the structure as well."

"Then by all means do." Acacia motioned toward the door.

Birk wasn't sure what she wanted with his scale, or how it would keep Lily safe, but he'd do as she asked. These women were that special.

After he shifted, he yanked out the scale and actually winced. Apparently, the area over the scar was still sensitive but maybe that was the point. He wasn't sure how long it would take, but the scale would grow back.

Birk shifted back and returned to the store. Primrose and Magnolia had joined the other two sisters. Magnolia, the eldest, took his scale. "This is too large to fit into the protection ring, so we'll have to grind it up. But don't worry. We'll make it into the shape of a heart and turn it into stone so no one will ever know what it's made out of. We'll then put a spell on it that will encompass the entire ring after it's been set. If Lily is ever in danger or afraid, all she has to do is rub a finger over the surface and that spot on your chest will vibrate. The heat will let you know that she needs you."

How clever. "That's perfect. Thank you." Even Lily wouldn't balk at that.

Magnolia carried the scale to the back room. When she returned, she was carrying a ruby colored stone, the same shade as his scale. It was remarkable. The four women placed the stone on the table and then each touched one corner. They closed their eyes and chanted in a strange language. If Birk didn't know how much they'd helped his family in the past, he might have thought they were crazy.

When they finished, they sprinkled herbs on top of the heart-shaped stone, said another incantation, and then handed it to him. "With this stone you will always know whether she is in trouble."

"I don't know how to thank you."

"You already have. Now be quick."

Their warning made him move swiftly. Once he was far enough away from the store, he held the stone tightly and shifted. If none of the SinCas jewelers were on site, he'd ask his brother Camden to fashion a ring for Lily.

Fortunately, Camden was there. Once he explained what he needed, his brother showed him a few settings.

"I like this one," Birk said. "It's delicate, like Lily."

"HOW DO YOU feel about Birk being your mate?" Kyle asked as he drank his hot tea.

Lily wanted to be honest with him and with herself. "I'm happy. I think. It's going to take some getting used to though. You know how I feel about dragon shifters."

"Still?" Her brother's eyes widened. "Do you feel differently about me now that I'm one?"

He was being silly. "Of course not. You're still my brother."

"And Birk is still, well, Birk." Kyle set down his cup and leaned forward in the chair, his elbows resting on his knees. "Let me ask you this. Has Birk ever done anything to make you afraid of him?"

"No. He's actually gone out of his way to be nice."

Kyle leaned back. "Then why not embrace the concept of being mates?"

When Lily had shown Birk her scarred back, he hadn't reacted like she'd expected, so she had no reason to fear any kind of rejection from him. Why wasn't she jumping for joy?

"Maybe I'm afraid Birk might not want to be with me after a while. He's gorgeous and strong and competent, and I have few skills." She wasn't anything like Kyle's mate, who not only was powerful, she had magic on her side.

"How about leaving that decision up to Birk? I've gotten to know him, and trust me, he won't become bored with you. Birk cares deeply for you—and I don't think it's just that Fate designated you as his mate."

Lily didn't understand any of this Fate stuff. "I hope that's the case."

Someone knocked and instantly a stab of fear shot through her until Kyle smiled.

"Relax. It's only Birk," he said.

"How do you know it's not some other dragon shifter come to harm me?" He'd told her he was able to detect all kinds of shifters.

"Now that I'm mated to Nessa, her sister and brothers all have the same vibration radiating off them."

That almost made sense. "Okay, but check the peephole first."

Kyle smiled. "Stop worrying." He made a big show of looking before opening the door. "Hey, Birk."

"Sorry, I took so long." Birk stepped past him and looked at Lily. "I had to make another stop on the way back here."

The room seemed to shrink, but instead of any discomfort coursing through Lily, she had a sudden urge to kiss him.

"No problem," Kyle said. "It gave Lily and me a chance to catch up." He slapped Birk on the back. "If you don't need me anymore tonight, I'll head on back to your sister."

Birk smiled, and her insides tumbled. She hadn't seen him this cheerful in a long time.

"Go, we're good."

Lily was curious where Birk had gone, but she'd wait for him to tell her. Instead of sitting, he remained standing. That didn't bode well.

"Are you up for some dinner?" he asked. "I'm starving."

So was she. Lily had turned him down for so many dates the word *no* was on the tip of her tongue. Only then did she realize she had no reason to deny him anymore. "You mean you'll let me out of my cave even though you think the world is about to attack me?" She waved a hand around her tiny apartment and then made sure to smile.

His eyes sparkled. "Yes, because I'll be with you. When we get to the restaurant, I'll even tell you where I went."

Excited for the first time in a while, she jumped up. "Let me get my purse and a sweater. Some restaurants are cold." Kyle had said it was because many dragon shifters were so hot blooded that the restaurant owners kept their establishments quite chilly.

Now that Lily had decided to give Birk a chance, she couldn't wait to have a real date—one where she didn't have to worry about him doing something she didn't want.

Chapter Eight

"TELL ME WHAT your favorite color is," Birk said once they were seated at the steakhouse.

Even though he'd ordered her favorite wine, a dry Mainsent, she vowed to keep it to one drink. Lily lifted the glass and sipped. "Hmm. My favorite color..." Her mind spun. "Maybe lime green?"

Birk smiled. "You don't know?"

She laughed. "I'm not sure anyone has ever asked me that question, though it shouldn't matter. I should know. What's yours?"

"Whatever color your scales turn out to be."

Lily wasn't sure how to respond, but the heat flushing her face should have convinced him that the topic of mating and turning into a dragon was an uncomfortable one. "Let's not get ahead of ourselves."

The light in his eyes dimmed. "You're right. I'm sorry."

Lily reached out and touched his hand. "I didn't mean it that way. It's just that I've never been in a good relationship before, so you'll have to excuse me if I do or say anything that seems...insensitive maybe?"

Birk smiled, and his eyes lit up once more, transforming his irises from brown to that pretty teal color. "You aren't capable of being insensitive, Lily."

"It's still early." Lily laughed, hoping to inject some humor into the slightly strained conversation.

"We'll see." Birk leaned back in his seat and then polished off his glass of wine. "Given you ordered salmon for dinner, am I to assume that is your favorite food?"

"Yes, it is." This time she didn't hesitate. She'd never seen this side of Birk before, but she liked it. "Something's going on with you. What is it?"

Birk placed a hand on his chest. "What do you mean? Can't I learn more about you?"

He had a point, but she doubted that was the reason for his questions. "Sure, but you seem different somehow. Was it because you told me we are mates?"

"That's a large part of it. Plus, you agreed to go to dinner with me. That's a huge victory."

She chuckled. Birk did seem genuinely excited to be with her. "I need to apologize once more. I shouldn't have assumed you'd be like the rest of the men I've known."

He set his empty glass back on the table and poured a refill. "How about we have a truce? No more apologizing, because I know I'm the one who will be making a ton of mistakes."

Lily loved that Birk seemed to be as nervous as she was about being together. "Deal."

"Good." Birk reached into his pocket and held out his fist. "When I left this evening, it was to have something special made for you." He unfolded his hand to expose a gorgeous ruby red stone ring that was in the shape of a heart.

She sucked in a breath. "I've never seen anything like it before. It's beautiful."

"It's called a protection ring." Birk described how he'd taken a ruby scale from his body and had it ground up fine. When mixed with some herbs, it turned into a stone. "Some special white-lighters put a spell on it to make that happen. I then had my younger brother, Camden, make it into a ring—which was what took me so long. If you rub the surface, I'll be able to tell if you're in distress." He handed it to her.

Lily had never heard of anything like that before. Then again, she wasn't friends with any white lighters—other than Nessa. Lily slipped it on her right hand and wiggled her fingers. "Perfect fit. Can

I test it out?"

"You can try, but since you aren't in any trouble, I might not sense anything."

She'd never been given such a special gift like this before. Actually, it wasn't the ring itself that was special as much as it was Birk. How had she been so blind before to lump him into the same category as Nelor?

Lily ran her thumb over the surface and then looked up at him. "Did you feel anything?"

He shook his head. "No, but as I said, I will if you're afraid. If you ever need me, and I'm not around, the ring will let me know I need to come for you."

She smiled, still in disbelief that something like this could work. "Thank you. I will." Lily nodded to his almost finished dinner. "Back to our twenty questions. Is steak your favorite food?"

Talking about her emotions was too unsettling. Listening to Birk would be much easier to deal with.

"Sometimes, but I like to change things up." He placed his napkin on his lap. "I have one for you. What was your favorite memory growing up?"

"That's easy. On my thirteenth birthday, my aunt took me to Earth."

His eyes widened. "At thirteen? I didn't go through the portal until I was close to forty."

His confession shook her for a minute until she remembered that dragons aged very slowly compared to humans. Birk had previously told her he was over one hundred years old, but he sure didn't look much older than thirty. "Now that you mention it, I think I would have appreciated visiting Earth a lot more if I had waited," she said.

"Where did you go?" Excitement laced his voice.

"To New York City. Growing up, I had always been a dreamer and loved to read. When the woman my aunt cleaned for gave her two tickets to the Broadway Show *Cats* as a thank you, my aunt knew she had to take me with her."

"Had she ever been to Earth before?"

"Twice. My uncle had been fairly well off, but he died rather young. When she ran through their savings, my aunt went back to work." Lily sighed. "In hindsight, I believe my aunt wanted to go more than I did." She let the memory wash over her. "I remember her being so nervous at having to apply for a portal crossing."

"Why? Usually, it's only criminals who have to worry about being denied."

"I know, but because she was a servant, she feared the guards would turn her down. She even had to ask for an advance—in dollars—to go." Lily waved a hand to erase that image. "Thankfully, we were granted entry. When we arrived, I was totally overwhelmed."

"By the number of people?"

"By everything—the noise, the smells, and even by the way people from Earth dressed. Not to mention there were no dragons buzzing overhead."

Birk nodded. "I had the same experience the first time I went, but my dad took me out west, so I wasn't overloaded with tall buildings or a massive amount of traffic. I did find the more often I went, the more things seemed to be the same as here. Those in the U.S. drive Fords and Chevys, while we drive Zandons and Ulrichs, but the concept for both is the same. For the most part, we Tarradonians have been heavily influenced by those on Earth."

"I hadn't been sure if that was true until I saw it for myself."

For a brief moment she thought about asking if he'd take her again, but Kyle said now that he was with Nessa, he could come and go to the other realms with no problem.

"Did you enjoy it?" he asked.

"Enjoy what?"

He laughed. "The play. My cousin Kaleena has mentioned a few times how she's always wanted to see a Broadway show."

"Yes, I loved it. It was all so magical." She chuckled at the memory. "After that, I became fixated on cats."

"The animal kind or the shifter kind?"

Lily was so enjoying Birk. This side of him was fun and interesting. "The animal kind, though it did make me wonder about shifters. Nelor was my first shifter, and you know how that turned out."

"All dragons were not created equally."

"I realize that now."

Their waiter came over. "Finished?" he asked.

"Yes," Birk said.

"Would either of you care for dessert?" he asked.

Birk was so fit that she bet he could eat ten desserts and not gain an ounce. Because she was short and sat at a desk for much of the day, just looking at cake put on the pounds. "I'm good," she said.

"Me too. The check please," Birk said.

Because he had asked her out, she suspected he'd want to pay. After he did and left a generous tip, Birk escorted her to the door. He then had her wait inside, while he went out and surveyed the street. Birk was an over-the-top bodyguard, but it gave Lily a sense of assurance that she was safe in his care.

He'd just escorted her to the car when his phone rang. "It's Declan," he said as he held open the car door for her to slide in. He pressed the phone to his ear. "What's up? We just left the steakhouse." Birk walked around the car to his side and hopped in, not saying anything for a minute. "I see. Thanks. Of course. See you there."

Birk stuffed the phone in his pocket but said nothing as he started the car. "What did he want?" she finally asked after Birk pulled onto the road.

"Apparently there has been a development, and Declan needs to discuss it with us."

Us? She didn't like the way his voice had turned hard. "Did he say what kind of development?"

"Not completely."

From the change in his mood, he'd told Birk something that wasn't good. Since he wasn't speeding home or glancing every few seconds into the rear view mirror, it probably wasn't anything life threatening.

Once they arrived at her place, he managed to find a spot in front of her apartment.

Birk reached out and gave her leg a quick squeeze, and his mere touch excited her. "Wait until I come over to your side before you get out."

Really? "The apartment building is all of twenty feet away."

He shrugged. "You know me. I can't be too careful. Humor me, okay?"

After the wonderful evening, she'd agree to almost anything. "Sure."

While he was taking this protection stuff too far, she understood his need. Kyle had explained what it was like being mated to Nessa. Every time his mate experienced a fast heart rate, he knew it. Yikes. She wasn't sure she was ready for that kind of intimate connection.

While Birk wasn't pressuring her to mate—for which she was grateful—he would ask her at some point. She appreciated that he had given her a choice whether to accept his offer of mating or not.

He opened the car door. "All clear."

When they stepped into her hallway, Declan was waiting for them. He nodded at both of them. "I trust you had a nice dinner?" He glanced between them, but clearly the question was directed at her.

"Yes. The food and conversation were excellent." She unlocked her door. "Come in. Can I brew you a cup of tea, Declan?"

"No, thank you. Unfortunately, this isn't a social call."

Okay, that wasn't good. Lily dropped her purse on the dining room table and slipped off her sweater. Declan sat in the chair, while she and Birk took the sofa across from him.

"Why don't you tell Lily what you told me," Birk said.

"Sure. Our cousin, Anderson Caspian, is a detective for the A.P.P. This afternoon, Thresh Toma turned himself in."

Lily's pulse soared. "For attempting to hurt me?"

His chin tucked in as if he knew nothing about that incident. "No, for burning down his warehouse."

"Why would he admit to something that will earn him jail time?"

Declan shot a look at Birk she couldn't quite decipher. Birk nodded and twisted toward her. "Toma has done a lot of things in his life that he's not proud of."

"I'll grant you that he's no saint." Though she assumed he'd never feel guilty about committing a crime. "Does he feel that bad about what he did?"

"I guess," Birk said.

"Why would he come forward now? He's been denying it the whole time."

"Remember you said that Mrs. Toma told you her ex-husband's last venture failed?"

"Yes."

"To keep things afloat, he had to borrow money—a staggering amount."

She could fill in the rest. "And whoever he borrowed the money from wants it back, so he torched his own warehouse to get it."

Declan leaned forward. "Mostly. Toma actually hired someone to do the deed, but he won't name anyone. That's not what worries us though."

"Then what?"

"When Toma realized he wouldn't receive all the money he needed, he tried his hand at gambling. Unfortunately for him, that didn't give him enough either. When the date they gave him to pay expired, some men kidnapped his daughters as collateral. They told him that their boss was willing to give him an extension to pay off the rest of the loan."

"Why turn himself in?"

"Toma now wants the police to help him get his daughters back. He gave them the name of the man responsible for the kidnapping. It's Richard Dorlack, a known syndicate boss who we've been trying to catch for a while."

"That sounds like good news. You know who has his daughters, and from what Birk said, he's in Glen Meadow, so why aren't you celebrating?"

Declan scrubbed a hand down his jaw. "Dorlack told Toma that he has ten days to pay him back. If he does, his daughters will be returned. If he doesn't, his daughters will be sold on the black market."

Lily sucked in a breath. She'd heard that kind of thing happening on Tarradon, but she'd never wanted to believe it was true. "He's hoping that by giving you Dorlack, the police would step in and save his family?"

"Yes and no," Declan said. "Toma received a call early this morning. Unbeknownst to him until now, Dorlack's men have had Toma under surveillance for quite some time. They spotted you going to his office and then checking out the warehouse."

She didn't see where he was headed, but dread was pooling in her stomach nonetheless. "And?"

"When Dorlack watched the video feed, he found you highly attractive."

That was the last thing she expected him to say. Birk grabbed her hand and squeezed hard, probably with more force than he'd intended.

"Why are you telling us this?" Birk said between gritted teeth.

Declan inhaled deeply then slowly let out his breath. "Because Dorlack told Toma that if he delivered Lily to him, he'd not only return his two daughters, he'd forget the debt Toma owes him."

Birk barked out a laugh while Lily's heart nearly stopped. "Does he really think Toma is capable of taking Lily? If he thinks that, then Dorlack is delusional," Birk said.

Lily was speechless. "Do you believe Toma?" She looked between Declan and Birk.

Declan nodded. "Toma knows Birk is your protector. Toma admits that while he didn't treat you with proper respect, he's not willing to assist in abducting you and turning you over to someone who would abuse you or worse."

Birk let go of her hand, wrapped an arm around her shoulders, and pulled her close. "If Dorlack decides to come after Lily himself, he'll get her over my dead body."

Chapter Nine

BIRK COULDN'T THINK straight. All he wanted to do was charge out of Lily's apartment, fly to Glen Meadows, and kill the son of a bitch. "Did Toma tell Dorlack no, or did he claim that Lily would be happy to be one of the man's slaves in exchange for his two daughters?"

Declan held up his hands. "Take it easy. Nothing is going to happen to Lily."

A sharp vibration stabbed his chest, followed by a blast of heat. It took him a moment to realize that Lily must be rubbing the ring. He looked down at her hands, and sure enough, she was dragging her thumb across the surface. At least the ring worked.

"Tell me," Birk demanded.

"Toma told Dorlack that he'd work on delivering Lily."

"What the fuck does that mean? He's not a dragon shifter. He can't possibly think he can get through me to Lily." When Birk looked over at her, she was looking up at him as if he was her only hope. Birk clasped her hand and brought it to his lips. "Don't worry, Lily, I won't let anything happen to you."

"I have a plan, and it involves Anderson letting Toma go free—for now," Declan said.

"What are you thinking?" Birk shot back.

"I'm still working on it, but it will entail using every available Guardian. We don't want Dorlack to become suspicious."

Lily squeezed his hand. "Who are these Guardians? Kyle mentioned something about them."

After spending time with her over dinner, and seeing her so

relaxed with him, Birk was convinced they would be mates at some point. It was time to tell her. "The Guardians are dragons who have been imbued with certain talents—magic, if you will—passed down for generations. Fate designated the Sinclairs and Caspians as the torchbearers so to speak. Our role is to protect those on Tarradon who need our help."

"I never would have guessed, but I can see now that it must be true. Since you all have jobs, how do you manage all this protection stuff too?"

He smiled. "We have a good team in place to take over when we have to fight."

"And my brother? Is he a Guardian now too?"

Birk nodded. "He is an amazing fighter and a real asset to the team. He chose to be with us."

Lily looked down at her hands for a moment. "What about Nessa, Greer, and Tory? Are they required to do battle?"

He could only hope she was projecting what might be required of her someday. "Not required, but most do. Women and men have their different strengths, but it's not like the human world where the men are necessarily more powerful."

"Oh."

They'd have to talk about this later. Lily didn't need anything more to stress over.

Declan stood. "I don't need to tell you to keep an eye on Lily. The rest of us will figure out our next move. Time is ticking." His cousin stepped over to Lily. "Listen to Birk. He has close to one hundred years of experience."

She tried to smile, but her lips faltered. "Thank you."

As soon as Declan left, Lily looked up at him. "Why did that man target me? He doesn't even know me."

Birk's heart broke. Lily was so beautiful and delicate, and yet she couldn't see it at all. "Take a look in the mirror. Any man would want you, but note, no one but your mate will have you."

"You are a good man, Birk Caspian."

His heart swelled at those words. "Even though I'm a dragon shifter?"

Lily glanced to the side. "Yes, even though you are a dragon who can shoot fire. I know now that you would never aim it at me."

"No, never." He considered that a huge victory. When Lily yawned, he could see the stress in her face. "If you could bring me a pillow and a blanket, I'll sack out on the sofa."

"You can't sleep in here."

Damn. Her tone suddenly changed. "Lily, listen, I'm not leaving you alone."

She held up her hands. "No, I mean the sofa is too small. Sleep in my bed and I'll sleep out here."

He smiled at her generous heart. "No can do. If Dorlack sends a few of his goons to snatch you, I need to be the first one they see."

She sighed. "Do you know if those men are dragons or regular shifters?"

He wasn't sure if he should tell her, but he believed in honesty. "Many of the men who are involved in human trafficking are dragons. Dorlack may or may not be one, but most of his minions are. When it comes to fighting, dragons can't be beat."

Lily looked around. "I need you refreshed in the morning, and I doubt you'll get any sleep here." A small smile lifted her lips and she wagged a finger at him. "And no, sharing my double bed won't be any better."

Birk wasn't sure why he cracked up, but the idea of Lily thinking along those lines bolstered his spirits. "You have a better idea?"

"No."

"How about going to the safe house?" he said.

Her shoulders sagged. "Ugh. While it is beautiful, there's no natural sunlight."

"You'd be safe."

"I'd be a prisoner," she shot back.

If he were Dorlack, he'd send a ton of men. "Then there is only one solution."

"What is that?" she asked, crossing her arms over her chest.

"Stay at my place. I have two bedrooms and excellent security."

"How long before you find this Dorlack person?" she asked.

"I don't know, but I imagine if we do nothing, Dorlack will sell Toma's two daughters."

"Shit."

Whoa. That was totally out of character for his sweet princess. However, he liked her backbone. "What will it be? Stay with me, or remain awake all night knowing I'll be tossing and turning on this way too small sofa?"

Lily chuckled. "You know how to hit low."

"I do."

"Fine, we can stay at your place, but come Monday, I'm going into work. You're welcome to come along, but it will be boring." She rubbed her ring, but he felt nothing. "I have this, remember?"

"Yes, but even if I shift immediately, it will take me time to reach you, assuming I know where you are."

Her brows scrunched. "There's no GPS thingy inside?"

That was a great idea. "No, but maybe I can have my brother fashion something that attaches to the side. I would like to know your precise location."

"Good." Lily stood. "I'll go pack."

LILY SHOULD BE afraid—well, okay, she was scared—just not of Birk. It made sense that if she stayed at his place, the men who wanted to abduct her would be harder pressed to find her. With a bit more pep, she packed her bag as quickly as possible. If she needed more clothes, she figured she could return.

With her case in hand, she walked into the living room where Birk was standing by the window looking out. "See anyone?" she asked, working hard to keep her tone light.

"No. I wish I knew what they were planning though."

Lily wasn't sure if she wanted to know. "I'm ready."

"How about we drive to my place in your car so you'll have it to get to work?"

"That's great, but what about your car?"

"I won't need it. If I do, I'll pick it up."

"Okay." Lily stuck her hand in her pocket and extracted the key. Birk slipped it from her fingers. "I'll drive."

She was about to say she was perfectly capable, but then she realized he was probably better at doing evasive maneuvers should the need arise. Fingers crossed they weren't. After leading her to the apartment entrance, Birk motioned she remain behind the door while he checked the area. Surprisingly, his protective nature didn't bother her this time. It actually helped calm her rather than frustrate her. Knowing this was more than a job to him also helped a lot too.

"We're good," he said as he led her to her car, his gaze constantly searching the sky and the surrounding area.

"I should walk around town wearing a halter top to expose my back. Then this acquaintance of Toma wouldn't want me."

"Lily." Birk drew out her name, and she noticed his tone had dropped low. "Don't say things like that. There are a lot of men who wouldn't care about your scars. You know I certainly don't."

For the first time since her scarring, she had to admit that Birk might be right.

Thankfully, the ride to Birk's condo was uneventful.

"Does your whole family live in condos?"

He quirked a brow. "No, but I do. Does that bother you?"

"Not at all, but you seem like the type to want your own place—separate from others."

He chuckled. "You mean, I'm not the social type?"

"No, but…"

He chuckled. "I get it. You're right. I would like a home away from it all, but I stay here for two reasons. One is that I am close to everything, and secondly, I don't spend much time here anyway. What about you? You live in an apartment."

"I'm only renting, because I can't afford a home."

"I see."

He helped her out, and then led her to the elevator to his floor. She wasn't sure what she expected his place to look like, but the sparsely decorated living room fit him—nothing like Nessa's that was well lit and decorated with an eye to excellence. Birk's was minimal at best, looking like an unused bachelor pad.

"I can see by the look on your face that you were expecting something a little more upscale," he said.

Oh, crap. Lily needed to work harder at controlling her facial expressions. "No. It's much bigger than my place."

He smiled. "The extra bedroom helps. Come on. I'll show you to the guest room."

For one second, she was tempted to ask to see his room. If he had a large bed, would it be to accommodate his size or did he share it often with women? It was stupid to think about those things now. If she believed Birk, she would be the only woman to ever share his bed again. At the thought, heat raced up her body.

Birk set down her suitcase and faced her. "Are you okay? You look a little flushed."

"I'm good." Oh, crap. He could read her mind. Or was it the damn ring? He smiled once more and her insides did a little dance.

"You have your own bathroom so you don't have to worry about sharing with me. Help yourself to anything in the kitchen, but I have to warn you, there's not much there."

"I'll be fine."

He set down her case by the door and then Birk clasped his hands behind his back. "I guess if you don't need me, I'll let you get settled."

As exhausted as she was, Lily didn't want to be alone. "I could use a glass of wine if you have any."

His brows rose. Birk was probably trying to decide whether he was invited to share a glass with her. "Let me check."

She wasn't sure if he expected her to stay in her room or follow him out. Talk about awkward. The cabinets banged, and she thought she heard a curse. A minute later, he returned. "Sorry. I'm fresh out. Tomorrow, we can shop, and we can pick up anything you want. How about a beer?"

She wasn't much of a beer drinker, but she didn't want to turn him down. "That's great. I'm guessing you eat out a lot?"

"Yes, most of the time."

When he'd been her bodyguard the last time, they'd stayed at the underground mine located on the Sinclair property, and the chefs had prepared their meals.

Lily stepped toward him, and it was as if some force lifted her hand to his chest. "Have I said anything to make you uncomfortable? You seem different around me now," she said.

Her heart beat harder in her chest as she awaited his answer.

"Yes, I'm different. Now that I've told you that you are my mate, it's all I can think about. Only another shifter can understand what it is like to be around the person Fate has paired him with." Birk looked away, but she didn't miss his fingers elongating and turning into talons.

"Birk?"

"Huh?"

She nodded to his hands.

"Oh, shit. Sorry. My dragon is acting up right now. The thought of us sleeping under the same roof—albeit in different rooms—has him a tad over-the-top excited."

Lily swallowed a smile. "Good to know."

Nessa had let a few things slip about how much she had wanted to be with Kyle, but it wasn't a topic Lily was very familiar with. "Is there something I can do? Like stay away from you?"

Birk huffed out a laugh. "Even when you aren't near me, you're still on my mind."

Lily was a bit shocked that he thought about her so much. "I would think that would be downright distracting when you're trying to do your job. How did all of this happen?"

Birk placed a hand on her head and stroked her hair. To her delight, his gentle touch soothed her, and she had to consciously refrain from moaning. Lily couldn't remember the last time a man touched her like that.

"All I can say is that the moment I walked into your apartment and saw you injured, lying on the floor, it was as if some invisible force invaded my body. This overwhelming urge to take care of you, wanting to be the only one near you or allowed to touch you, suddenly overtook all of my thoughts."

That caused more questions to surface. "What if you'd seen me at a restaurant or shopping with friends? Would you have had the same reaction? Or was it my injured state that caused you to feel this way?"

He smiled. "No. Once Fate decides it is time for me to meet my mate, it just happens. It could be at the grocery store or on a blind date."

That made her feel better. She certainly didn't want him to think they belonged together because she needed his protection. "Good to know."

Birk ran his hand over her shoulder and around to her back. "I'll grab those drinks, and then we can sit in the living room for a bit. And chat."

Lily wasn't able to tell whether this would be a serious talk about why he needed to hover over her, or if he just needed to explain a few more things.

Once he retrieved two beers, she followed him to the black leather sofa. He motioned she sit. Birk twisted off the cap and handed her the bottle. She thought it cute that it didn't occur to him that she might like a glass.

He angled toward her. "What about you?"

"What about me?"

He looked down at his hands for a moment. "Do you feel anything for me?"

Her chest nearly caved. She never thought this gorgeous, strong man would have an ounce of insecurity. "Of course, I do. Since I'm now past my insecurities about your reaction to seeing my back, I've been able to acknowledge my feelings. I care about you—a lot."

He leaned closer, his brows pinched. "Is it because you feel safe with me?"

Lily wasn't sure how to answer. Did she have the courage to say she'd grown to care for him more than she thought was possible? "I feel safe with you, yes, but it's more than that."

When Birk cupped her face, she nearly melted. "Tell me."

This was so embarrassing. "You're very attractive."

His eyes widened slightly. "I'll take attractive. Anything else?" He let go of her face and held up a hand. "I'm only asking because I don't want to move too fast."

"Oh, no," she said too quickly. "I'll tell you the moment you do something that makes me uncomfortable."

Birk smiled and her whole body lit up from the inside. "Then how about if I do this?"

As she was trying to figure out what *this* was, Birk leaned over, tilted her head back, and kissed her.

Chapter Ten

F ROM HER LIPS, straight down to her heated core, unexpected waves of desire swamped Lily. Holy shit. Never in her wildest dreams had she imagined Birk's lips would be so soft, yet so strong. And she certainly didn't expect her head to spin and her body to catch on fire—figuratively, not literally. When he let up on the pressure, she grabbed his head to keep him close. His eyes glowed teal, and she swore she caught flashes of ruby red out of the corner of her eyes.

It was only when he dragged a hand down her arm and brushed her breast that her instincts kicked in and made her stop.

"Okay, that was…nice," Lily said, ashamed she couldn't truly say that he'd melted her body down to her toes.

Birk's breath came out fast, and when he licked his lips, he closed his eyes for a moment as if he wanted to savor the kiss a minute longer.

"I would have used the word amazing or incredible." Birk flashed a smile, and then stood. "Lily, if I don't stop right now, I'm not sure I can control myself."

She didn't believe that. Birk seemed to be the epitome of self-control, but she couldn't call him a liar. "Goodnight then."

"I need you to go to bed too."

"Because you think someone will come in? I thought the purpose of having an eye scanner was to prevent anyone from entering." He sucked in his bottom lip. Clearly her logic was sound, but he needed her to be tucked away, so she held up a hand and then stood. "You know what? You're right. I am tired. I'll take a shower and turn in."

His jaw tightened, and then his eyes returned to the yummy brown color she liked. "Thank you."

While she really didn't understand his concern, he was doing her a favor by carefully watching over her, and she needed to show him that she appreciated all he was doing for her.

When she reached the bedroom door, which happened to be next to his, she faced him. "Thank you again for everything."

"You're welcome. Sleep well, Lily," he said while not quite looking her in the eye.

Frustrated at his sudden change, and a little upset at herself for breaking off the kiss so fast, she closed her door, grabbed some stuff from her suitcase, and then headed into the bathroom to shower. The moment she flicked on the lights, she sucked in a breath. She certainly hadn't expected the granite covered walls or the exquisite blown glass vessel sink. Never would she have guessed the place would have a massive shower with two showerheads either. Was this the master or were both bathrooms the same?

Like Birk, this condo was a contradiction. He exuded self-control and confidence, yet he was hesitant around her. From what Kyle had told her, Birk was amazing at his job, yet to her he appeared distracted all the time. She hoped it wasn't because of her that his inner dragon was causing him to lose focus. Nessa had let it slip that she too had been out of sorts until Kyle and she had become intimate. At first, her emotional upheaval had been bad, but it slowly improved.

Clearly, Lily had an awful lot to learn about dragon shifters. Her ex-boyfriend's behavior must have been atypical because while he claimed he liked her, he'd been lying.

The more she thought about mating with Birk—or at least seeing where the relationship would go—the more Lily liked the idea. The memory of the kiss filtered into her mind once more, causing a wave of lust to attack her. Damn, Birk. She wanted him but was afraid to take what he had to offer.

Shaking her head at her daydreaming, Lily undressed and

stepped into the shower. After setting the temperature button to moderate heat, she swiped her hand over the sensor to indicate which jets she wanted. Only once before, had she seen anything this fancy, and that had been on a business trip when she stayed at an upscale hotel.

Stepping under the hot flow, she soaped up and imagined what it would be like to see Birk naked. Her body rejoiced at that thought, hardening her nipples and making her inner walls spasm. Jeez. Now wasn't the time to think about falling for a man when her life was at stake. No, if nothing else, Lily Harper was an expert at pushing aside her emotions. Damn. It had been so pleasant to think how it could be with Birk.

She smiled at the memory of how desperate he seemed to be with her. That kiss! Oh, my. As clichéd as it sounded, her toes tingled—as did a few other body parts.

It had happened slowly, but Birk had won her over with his patience and kindness. And to think it hadn't been long ago that she felt stifled by him. Now, she enjoyed his company, especially after he explained why he was so protective. His concern and warmth sure had melted her cautious heart.

What sounded like water turning off in the room next door reminded her she wasn't alone in the condo. After she finished rinsing, Lily stepped out of the shower and enjoyed his fluffy towels. Birk would never cease to surprise her.

After changing into her comfy cotton pajamas, Lily crawled into bed. It might be late, but she wasn't ready to sleep. Because reading would take her mind off her troubles, she turned on her phone and chose a book. It wasn't long before the story totally swept her away into a fantasyland.

Lily had no idea how long she'd been reading, but a sound coming from the living room startled her, and every physical reaction claimed her—from the fast beating heart to the tightening of her chest, and then to the clamminess on her skin.

"Birk?" she called out. Her voice came out a croak.

When he didn't answer, she went to investigate. He'd assured her no one could gain access to his condo. It was on the 7th floor and didn't have a terrace, which meant no dragon could land and come in. As for the main door, no animal could penetrate it, and the eye scan prevented anyone from opening it.

She had to conclude Birk was the one in the living room rummaging around, and that her overactive imagination was going crazy. Knowing she wouldn't sleep until she looked, Lily opened the door a crack but found only darkness.

Another creak sounded, erasing all of her assurances from a moment before.

"Lily, is that you?" Birk asked.

Relief washed through her. As soon as she stepped from her room, the kitchen light clicked on. "I thought I heard something," she said.

"I'm sorry." He rushed up to her. "I was getting a drink. Would you like some water?"

"Water would be fine."

With his back turned to her, she couldn't help but admire his cute butt that was outlined nicely in his thin pajama bottoms.

"You couldn't sleep?" Tension laced his tone.

"I was reading."

As soon as he turned around, Lily couldn't take her eyes off his incredibly naked chest. When he'd shown her his scar before, she hadn't been in the right frame of mind to notice how hot he was. Nelor was a large man, but Birk was packed with twice as many muscles and was several inches taller. When he lifted the glass to hand it to her, his pectorals flexed. Oh, my.

Birk smiled. "Maybe I should put on a shirt," he said, but she could hear the pleasure in his tone.

"No need." Lily finally looked up at him, and heat flushed her face. She quickly drank the water, needing the cool liquid to calm her.

"Okay then. I'm going to try to get some shuteye," Birk said with a sudden playfulness in his tone.

She was tempted to ask him to stay a bit and talk to her, but she was a coward. "Goodnight."

While she'd seen his eyes flash teal when he glanced at her fairly thin pajama top, he didn't try to kiss her again. What was wrong with the man? She didn't think she'd ever understand him. He told her he wanted her worse than anything, and yet when she was within reach, he did nothing.

Oh, yeah. She'd been the one to break off the kiss, mostly because her reaction to his kiss surprised her.

As Birk strutted toward his room, she admired his finer than fine ass. His back muscles rippled, but she couldn't tell if it was due to tension or if he was flexing for her.

Should she go in after him? Or let him have his rest? If he wanted her so much, maybe he'd come into her room.

Aargh. Just as he was about to close his door, he twisted toward her. "I know you were checking out my ass." He winked, and heat flushed her face once more.

As much as she wanted to throw back a denial, her lips wouldn't move, though her jaw did drop a little.

Birk closed the door and then pushed it back open an inch. "The light switch is right here. Turn it off when you're done."

"Okay."

"In case you get scared again, I'll leave this open."

Was that an invitation? His footsteps moved across the hardwood floors, and then the bed squeaked. Lily still hadn't moved since her mind couldn't stop racing. What did she want to do? Get lost in the comfort of his arms or not? She'd slept alone for years but found little pleasure in it.

While Birk had the opportunity to seduce her when he was her bodyguard, he'd never even hinted that he liked her, so maybe his flirty comment about her checking out his hot body was his way of showing he wanted her to make the next move.

Go in!

As if some spirit was sitting on her shoulder urging her to take the plunge, she walked toward his door. She flicked off the living room light and was instantly bathed in darkness. At least with his room being dark, he wouldn't have to look at her back despite Birk claiming he didn't care about her scars.

Aw, what the hell. If she changed her mind, she'd tell him she wasn't ready and return to her room. Inhaling, she pushed open his door just far enough to slip in. Her breathing came out raspy in the silent night—or maybe it was her heart banging against her rib cage that caused the blood to pound in her ears.

"I won't bite," Birk said with humor in his tone.

Shit. She thought she could sneak in. How had she forgotten he was a dragon shifter with exceptional eyesight and hearing? "I know."

Birk changed positions and then turned on the nightstand light. "I don't want you to bang your toe or shin."

Her eyes must have widened. "Thank you." Okay, this was awkward. "I'm usually not this forward," she said, though Lily wasn't sure she really needed to explain.

"You're not being forward, at least not to me. We belong together, so it's natural that we enjoy each other."

His being nice helped calm her nerves. His teal eyes flashed and glowed, and his ruby colored scales pulsed under his skin. "Does it hurt?" she asked.

"Does what hurt?"

"When your scales glow like that?" Nessa had told her it happened when she was either angry or sexually excited, but she never commented on whether it was painful.

"No. Would you like to feel them? I need to warn you though that they emit a lot of heat."

Her blood pressure dropped at his casual tone. "Okay."

Birk scooted over to make room, and she crawled onto the bed. His small smile boosted her confidence.

She touched his abs where the color was coming from. His body was hot, and her body instantly turned into an inferno. "You are most definitely a dragon."

He chuckled. "I hope so. Come here, sugar." He gathered her into his arms and stretched out onto his back.

She had no choice but to place her head on his shoulder. When she inhaled his scent, which seemed to be a combination of pine and lemon, something stirred deep inside her. His inner dragon scales flashed again, and she automatically touched them. "They really are warm."

"The longer you are by my side, the hotter I become."

His flattery was so refreshing. Since Birk didn't seem to be in any hurry to make out, she decided to enjoy him. When she stroked the fine hairs on his chest, she couldn't help but moan.

As if he too was enjoying the prelude, Birk reached up and ran a hand down her hip, and his gentle touch set off something inside her that shut down all her inhibitions.

"I want you, Lily." As much as she had the urge to say she wanted him too, that final step was hard. Birk tilted her face toward his. "Kiss me."

She melted at his gentle command. Her mouth opened, and Birk leaned forward and cupped her face. When their lips touched, she could no longer hold back. For the first time in her life, it didn't seem to matter that he was a dragon shifter or that her back was burned. This was Birk—the man Fate had decided would be with her for the rest of her life, and that notion infused her with joy.

Wanting to show him how much she wanted to make love with him, Lily joined her tongue with his and leaned into his body more fully. His huge hard cock shouldn't have caught her off guard, but it did. Without thinking, she reached between them and pressed her hand against his shaft.

He grunted. "Lily, you're killing me. I want to go slowly, but my dragon is clawing my insides to take you."

"Then listen to your dragon."

Oh, my God, I didn't just say that!

He swung her onto her back and crawled on top, resting his

powerful body on his elbows. Birk closed his eyes and inhaled. "I want to take my time, I really do, but damn, I am working so hard to control myself right now."

She wasn't sure how to respond, so she reached up, tugged on his head, and kissed him once more. This time, it was Birk who slipped his tongue into her mouth, and the foray was sensual, pleasurable, and oh so exciting. Every tongue twist sent heat straight between her legs. Lily couldn't believe how Birk's touch ignited her so.

Before she was ready to stop, Birk broke the kiss and slipped downward.

"I have to taste you," he said as he undid the buttons on her pajama top and then lay open the fabric. "My dragon is clawing to break free."

She grabbed his arms. "I hope that's a figure of speech."

He smiled. "I hope so too, but he's on the same page as my human side. We have wanted you for so long that I don't trust him to stay put. I am working really hard to keep him pushed back and let me have the lead here."

Birk leaned over, and when he licked her nipple, she thought she'd be the one who might explode. Even through her pajama bottoms, her scent perfumed the air. Lily had never experienced such overwhelming need before. It was as if some white lighter had invaded her body and made her connect with him.

Massaging her other breast while he made love to her nipple with his mouth, Lily floated, thrilling to the joy coursing through her. She reached down and threaded her fingers through his short hair, and then pressed her palm against his scalp. The added pressure made Birk flick his tongue faster and faster. He reached between her legs and pressed his palm against her pussy.

Just as she was about to come, Birk released his hold on her and dropped between her legs. Lily damned him and cheered him at the same time. She closed her eyes in anticipation of the onslaught of glorious bliss.

"These have to go." When he tugged on her bottoms, she lifted up, and they became history.

"Much better," she said.

He licked her once and then sucked in an audible breath. "Mmm. You even taste as sweet as sugar."

Every preconceived notion about men and how unfeeling and uncaring they were, flew out the window. She wiggled her butt against the cool sheets and clamped her hands on his shoulders, willing him to continue to feast on her. "Go ahead and satisfy your sweet tooth."

He chuckled, but she'd been deadly serious. To her delight, he did continue. In fact, each lick and suck pushed her closer to the brink of that climax. When he sucked on her clit however, she could no longer stop her orgasm from claiming her.

Lily sucked in a breath and dug her nails into his skin. "Yes!" she shouted.

Birk pressed his cheek against her pussy and sighed. "I think bringing you pleasure is my new favorite pastime."

He held her tight, probably waiting for her breathing to slow down before continuing. Her fingers finally uncurled, and her body slowly relaxed into the bed. Only then was she able to speak. "I'd like to do the same for you."

Birk lifted his head and then shook it. "I don't think so, sugar. I'm hanging on by a very thin thread and don't have that much control right now. Trust me—I look forward to you returning the favor next time."

She grunted her disapproval. "Can I at least help release that dragon in your pants?"

Birk cracked up and then rolled onto his back. "Sure. I'll never turn down an offer from you, especially when you want to light my fire, my beautiful woman."

Lily had no idea where this witty, funny guy had been all these past weeks, but she was enjoying the repartee now. Birk slipped his pants off partway. "You said I could do that." She tried to sound disgruntled.

He lifted his hands. "Fine, but you need to be quick."

Something overtook her mind, because as soon as she dragged his pajama bottoms down, she leaned over and swiped her tongue along his length.

"Oh, no you don't," he said.

A second later she was flat on her back with Birk hovering over her.

Chapter Eleven

B IRK WAS ABOUT to break. Having Lily in his arms was more amazing and wonderful than he could have ever imagined. If he messed things up now, he'd never forgive himself.

To his delight, his flirty comebacks seemed to please her, and for the first time in maybe forever, tension wasn't twisting his muscles into knots.

She tapped his forehead. "Where did you go, dragon-boy?"

He smiled at the nickname. "Just thinking how incredible you are."

She cocked a brow. "Showing is a lot more convincing."

Where Lily's sudden confidence had come from, he didn't know, but he sure as hell liked it. He'd detected the change in her when he told her they were mates. Having grown up without a dad might have caused her to be cautious around men—that, and that asshole Nelor turning on her.

The idea of having someone around forever must have appealed to her. When her lips parted, he leaned over and kissed her. Hard. Passionately. Seductively.

Mate, mate, his dragon said, cheering him on.

I need to take it slow.

Then why are you devouring her?

Birk lightened up on the kiss and swirled his tongue around hers instead of probing deeply, but he found it difficult not to want to take all of her. He delved into her sweet mouth again, and then nudged open her legs with his knee, waiting for her to tell him she wasn't ready.

It must have been his lucky day because Lily planted her feet on the bed and lifted her hips. That completely unraveled him. Now, he had to have her.

Heat slammed through his veins as his ruby scales flickered and pulsed. Needing to test the waters, he slipped his cock between her legs and stopped at her entrance.

"Birk, please, take me now."

That was all he needed to hear. Using all of his control, he slid into her eager pussy and nearly shifted when he reached the end. As wild lust grabbed him hard, his breath caught. This was his mate, the woman he would love and protect forever.

She tried to move beneath him, but he drew his knees inward to keep her still. "Give me a second, please."

Lily stopped moving but then cupped his face and drew him close enough to make love to his mouth. It was too much. With her breasts pressed against his chest, her heat wrapped around his cock, and her tongue about to tangle with his, Birk was unable to keep from retreating and then driving back into her.

His balls drew up tight, and his cock and tongue plunged into her again and again. He savored her sweetness, and Lily moaned and dug her nails into his shoulders. Sweat beaded their bodies as they fucked hard and with total abandon.

Lily broke the kiss. She let out a scream as her eyes rolled back in her head. He'd never been more turned on. When her inner walls clamped down hard on him, his hot cum detonated.

"Oh, Lily."

A long while later, Birk rolled over and dragged her on top, where she lay with her cheek on his chest, while he remained snug inside her. Wrapping his arms around her, he kissed her forehead, never wanting to let her go.

He said nothing until her breathing slowed. "Shit! I'm so sorry, Lily. I was caught up in the moment that I forgot to use protection."

She patted his chest. "It's okay. I've taken precautions. Not only am I on the pill, I was checked out after Nelor."

Part of him was disappointed. He wanted heirs, but that would come later. "Smart. I'm good to go too."

Finally, she lifted her head. "We need to clean up."

"I'll find us something." He rolled her to the side and slipped out of her. In the bathroom, he wet a washcloth to clean her up first and then himself. Once he tossed the cloth back into the sink, he crawled into bed. "Will you stay the night with me—in my bed?"

Lily snuggled against him and sighed. "Yes."

BIRK HELD THE phone to his ear and watched Lily grab a glass from the kitchen cabinet and hold it under the faucet. "I'll ask her, but what do you plan to do, Ness?"

"Before the A.P.P. turns Toma loose, I thought we'd take her out for a girl's day. Maybe the four of us will have a little makeover session, catch a movie, or go shopping. We're not sure."

The water turned off and Lily moved toward him. It was Saturday, so she thankfully wasn't working today. He turned his back to her and lowered his voice. "What if Toma's men come after her?"

Nessa huffed. "We'll stick to the main part of the city. I'm sure that Tory, Greer, Kaleena, and I can handle them. Remember, four is better than one, and we are Guardians, my dear brother."

That was true. Furthermore, Declan had called and said that he, Kyle, and Finn were heading to Glen Meadow again today to look for Toma's daughters. He'd even asked if Birk was free to help.

"I'm sure she'll be happy to join you four. Will you pick her up here or should I drop her off?"

"I'll pick her up."

"Let me ask Lily." Birk pressed the phone to his chest. "Nessa, Greer, Kaleena, and Tory would like to take you out for the day. Would you like to go?"

"Are you coming?"

He couldn't tell if she wanted him to. "I'm not invited. It's a girls-only thing. Don't worry—you'll be safe with them if that's your concern."

"What are you going to do?"

"Help Declan find Toma's daughters."

Lily pressed her lips together possibly indicating she wasn't pleased he might be putting his life in danger, but then she smiled. "Yes, I'd love to go."

It would be good for her to be out and about and not have to worry about anything. He lifted the phone. "Lily would be thrilled."

"We'll pick her up soon."

"Good." He disconnected.

"What's the occasion?" she asked.

"I don't know. I'm guessing it's to give you a break from me."

Lily came over to him with her glass in hand. The nearer she drew, the more his body heated. "I don't need a break from you, but getting to know your sisters and cousins will be nice."

"Thank you, and I agree. They are fun." He held up a finger. "Even though all four women can defend you, be alert at all times."

When Lily laughed, he was tempted to seduce her again.

"WHAT DO YOU think?" the hairdresser asked Lily as she turned her toward the mirror to see the final product.

"I look so different." Lily's heart fluttered at the woman staring back at her. She fingered her trimmed hair that had been highlighted with darker brown streaks. She twisted her head to the right and then the left, loving how her slightly curly hair swished on her shoulders. "I like it." She turned toward Nessa. "What will Birk think about it?"

Nessa, Kaleena, and Greer had their hair done already and were huddled around her. Nessa fingered Lily's hair. "Birk is going to love it. Though I bet even if you'd opted to shave your head, he'd tell you how hot you looked."

Okay, that was a worrisome comment. "Are you saying Birk isn't always truthful?"

"Never! It's just that Birk will think you are beautiful no matter what. It's who he is."

Lily genuinely smiled. "Good to know."

Nessa turned to the other three women. "Who's up for takeout at my place?"

"I'm in," Kaleena said. "Finn is with Birk, so I'm totally free for the evening."

Tory raised her hand. "You don't have to ask me twice."

Greer turned to her sister. "I'm game, but you know I don't drink a lot."

Lily liked Greer in part because she was the quiet one of the bunch. If she didn't know Greer was a dragon shifter, she never would have guessed. From an outsider's perspective, Greer just wanted to sell jewelry—not fight evil forces.

"Great," Nessa said.

Once Lily paid the stylist, she gathered the sexy clothes the girls insisted she purchase and walked out with them. It was comforting how the four of them surrounded her, making sure a dragon shifter protected her on all four sides.

When Lily stepped outside and noticed the sun was setting, she hadn't realized how long they'd been in the salon. The pinks and purples of the sky reflected off the glass buildings, lighting up the downtown, making for an absolutely gorgeous view. Add in the fact that the evening air was clear and crisp, and Lily could almost forget that anyone wanted to harm her.

Once they all piled into the car, Nessa took off.

"So Lily, what was the best part of the day for you?" Tory asked.

She couldn't possibly answer that. Kaleena had spearheaded the shopping spree, Nessa the hair salon, and Greer the makeup redo. Lily decided to stay on safe ground. "The fact you all asked me to join you and then protected me with your lives."

All of the women smiled. Nessa glanced in the rear view mirror at her. "What food are you in the mood to eat, Lily?"

Why was she asking her? Sure, she felt like the guest of honor, but the others should have a say so. "I'm good with anything."

"Pizza okay then?"

"It's one of my favorite foods." That was the truth.

"I'll call it in as soon as we get home."

It didn't take long before they were parked in a garage under Nessa's condo. After Tory did a quick sweep of the area for anyone lurking about, she returned. "All clear," she said as she opened the back door for Lily to exit.

Just like Birk's, her condo had an eye scanner. Maybe Lily should ask him to install one of those at her place since it would give her a feeling of safety.

Once inside, Nessa took orders and called for pizza delivery while Kaleena asked what everyone wanted to drink. Greer sat next to Lily while Tory grabbed the plates and napkins. She then plopped everything down on the oversized coffee table that separated the two sofas.

"How is it going with my brother?" Greer asked with a lot of excitement in her voice.

She wasn't about to say he was an amazing lover. "Good. After he told me I was his mate, he calmed down a bit—or else I understood better why he was so protective all the time."

Greer chuckled. "Birk always has worried about others. You're lucky Fate paired you with him."

"I know that now, but at first I thought I was the unluckiest person in the realm to have a dragon shifter around me all the time."

Greer patted her hand. "I'm sorry what happened with your last boyfriend. All species have bad ones."

Wasn't that the truth?

Nessa pocketed her cell and sat down next to Tory on the sofa across from where Lily and Greer were sitting. Kaleena placed the drinks in front of everyone and sat in one of the chairs flanking the two sofas.

"Lily, do you have any questions for us?" Nessa asked.

"Questions?"

She smiled. "Like what might happen after you and Birk mate—unless of course Kyle filled you in already? I know he originally had a lot of concerns before we mated."

"I haven't spoken to him since Birk told me we are mates, but he gave me a general rundown. I'm sure at some point I'll be asking you all kinds of stuff." Lily held up a finger. "I do have a question for Kaleena though."

"Ask away."

"How did you and Finn meet? I've heard bits and pieces but not the whole story." In part, she wanted to learn if the way mates were paired was the same for everyone.

Her eyes widened slightly. "I can't believe you don't know." Kaleena leaned forward and picked up her glass. "For starters, I need to tell you that I've known Finn was my mate for many years."

"For years? Birk told me he had no idea we were fated to be together until Nessa and he came into my apartment."

Kaleena smiled. "That's true, but I have a unique talent in that I can dream-walk." She explained in more detail what that meant. "So after I was captured by my cousin, Prince Rathan, I told Finn—who was on Earth at the time—that I was in trouble. It was how he knew to come here."

"That was very brave of him. Did he know you were a dragon shifter?" Lily wondered if she was the only one who had been afraid of them.

Kaleena shook her head. "No. I thought if I told him, he might fear me."

Aha. "Obviously, Finn found a way to locate the portal and come here, but how was a wolf shifter able to sneak into the castle and save you?"

She smiled. "He had a lot of help from my family and the Four Sisters of Fate." She detailed all that was involved in getting him inside and finding the cells.

"Wow. I know white lighters are powerful, but I had no idea

those sisters could do that."

Kaleena nodded. "They are amazing, and the rescue itself was equally as impressive."

"Weren't you scared being cooped up like that?"

"Very much so—I was forced to wear cuffs that sent poison into my system, and then took away my ability to shift or do magic. But that wasn't the worst part."

Losing her powers was hard to relate to, but Lily could empathize with how troubling it must have been for someone like her. "What was the worst part?" Lily picked up her glass of wine and sipped it.

"Not being able to help the others who were imprisoned alongside of me. While I can't be positive, some were white lighters like me. They had done nothing wrong other than possess magic."

"That's horrible and so unjust. Were any of them dragon shifters?" Lily asked.

"I couldn't be sure."

"Can't your family save them?" Lily couldn't imagine being held prisoner if she'd done nothing wrong.

"Our fathers are working on the logistics now." Kaleena looked over at Tory and then Nessa.

"A rescue is highly dangerous," Tory said. "If anything goes wrong, there would be a lot of bloodshed. The king's men might not possess as much magic as we do, but they are highly trained. Birk's brother, Thane, works hard to train us, but we don't spend hours each day training like the Royals do."

"But Finn found his way in there before. Why can't he do that face thing again?"

Kaleena smiled. "The sisters don't like to interfere with the path Fate has set for some people."

"I see." Lily wished she could help, but she had no special abilities. She would have to speak with Birk, hoping he had some ideas.

The doorbell rang, and Nessa jumped up. She checked the security hole before opening the door. "Pizza's here."

After paying, Nessa carried in the meal. Unless these women ate as much as Birk, there was no way they'd finish this much food.

"Dig in," Nessa said.

They each grabbed a slice of pizza and a bread stick. After a few bites and a lot of appreciative moans, Lily asked what each of them did in the family business. They went around and explained what their role was. Lily found it interesting and impressive how capable and smart these women were.

Lily wiped her mouth. "What's fascinating is how different you all are. And to think you're related."

The four women glanced at each other. "Don't let the fact that I work at the retail end of the business fool you," Greer said. "While I am a healer, as you and your brother both found out, I can and do fight when needed, though I prefer to help in other ways."

That was a surprise.

Kaleena nodded. "Greer may be elegant and controlled, but she is a powerhouse against evil."

Nessa chuckled. "One more thing. Just because Greer dresses like a lady, whereas I go around wearing baggy miner's clothes, don't underestimate her."

Lily held up her hands. "Thanks for the warning."

Everyone was quiet for a moment until Greer held up her nearly full glass. "To fooling some people all of the time and all of the people some of the time."

Lily laughed. "Do all dragons more or less look alike?"

The women glanced at each other. This time Tory spoke. "Everyone in our family has different colored scales that are interspersed with the black ones, but there are other differences, such as the shape of the snout and the spacing of the spikes on the back of the tail. Stuff like that. When you become a dragon, you'll be able to tell one from the other more easily."

When she became a dragon? That was a scary thought, though an inevitable reality.

Kaleena held up a finger. "We should mention that while we

don't have a choice in what we are born with, it seems as if the more dominant family members end up with colors in the red family. Declan's scales are a rather bright red whereas Birk's are more ruby. Sometimes, even I have mistaken those two.

Interesting. "Will my scale colors match Birk's then?"

"No," they said in unison. "It's not like human DNA where you inherit physical traits."

"I see." Kind of.

Tory asked her about her work, and the discussion went downhill from there once the serious drinking began.

After another hour of conversation, Nessa polished off the last of the pizza. "Anyone up for watching some movies with hot sex going on?"

The women all talked at once. Apparently, as long as Nessa made her famous popcorn, they didn't care what she picked.

Chapter Twelve

THE LAST FEW texts Birk had sent to Nessa had gone unanswered. Given it was close to ten at night, Birk was beginning to worry. Sure, Lily wore the ring that would send him a message if she were afraid, but what if she were unconscious and unable to rub the ring?

She's fine, his dragon said, sounding rather exasperated at his worrying.

How can you be so sure?

I would have sensed it.

He could almost visualize his animal lifting his haughty head. Enough was enough. Birk was going over to his sister's place to pick up Lily, and he didn't care how much anyone complained. He wasn't going to take a chance that something had happened to her. So what if she was surrounded by four very competent dragon shifters—shifters who happened to be Guardians and were trained by the best?

His anxiety might have stemmed from the fact he and the men were no further along in determining the scope of the human trafficking ring run by Richard Dorlack. Birk couldn't chance the ass might have already sent ten shifters after Lily.

Birk and Nessa lived quite close, so he chose to walk—or rather jogged—over to his sister's place. He entered through the parking garage instead of through the main entrance to make sure Nessa's car was parked in her usual spot. It was. Birk shouldn't be so concerned, but when it came to his mate, he couldn't help it.

As soon as he stepped off the elevator at her floor, laughter floated down the hallway, and the tension in his shoulders released somewhat. He recognized Tory's and his sister's voices, but not Lily's. Birk debated turning around since he didn't want to interrupt her good time, but it was possible Lily might want to leave—not to be with him necessarily, but because she was tired.

Or was Birk just being selfish? Whatever. He was a shifter in need. After waiting a minute at the door and never hearing Lily's voice, he finally knocked.

The sound from the television was still blaring when Nessa answered. "Well, well, if it isn't my brother! Come for Lily?"

"You know I have."

Nessa grinned and motioned him in. "Fun's over girls. The big bad dragon is shutting us down."

Lily stood and then giggled. "Be kind, Nessa. I'm sure Birk was worried about me. I have been gone all day, and you know how anxious he gets." She held up a glass of wine and polished it off.

Tory and Kaleena were still glued to whatever was on the large screen. When Birk glanced over at it, he sucked in a breath. Holy shit, it was two naked men having sex with a woman.

Tory hummed. "Oh, my. He is very well hung, isn't he?" She swayed right and left.

Kaleena grinned. "Let's just say I've seen as big."

"Oooh," Tory said. "Better keep your mate close by your side in that case."

"I plan to." Kaleena laughed.

Lily wove her way over to Birk, waving her now empty glass. "Hey there. Hope you weren't *too* worried." With her free hand, she dragged a finger down his chest straight to his cock.

His body nearly exploded. "How much have you had to drink?" Her breath smelled fruity.

Her smile widened. "I lost track."

Not sure what to say, he just stared at Lily. While he loved her look before, the new hairdo and makeup had his libido skyrocketing. Even his talons threatened to poke through his skin.

She spun around, her scent swirling inside him and making his dragon growl in anticipation. "Do you like the new me?" she asked.

"I'll get your shopping bags, Lily, from the spare bedroom," Nessa said with a huge grin. Damn. His eyes must have turned turquoise.

Sure enough, when he glanced down at his arms, his ruby red scales were shining through his clothes.

"I love it." Almost too much, Birk thought to himself as he ran his tongue along his teeth—teeth that had sharpened to points. Damn.

Lily leaned into him and then cupped his balls in front of everyone. Heat raced up his body. "Want to have some fun?"

Enough was enough. He lifted Lily's hand off his crotch. "I'm taking you home."

She giggled. "I hope to bed."

"Shh." If she kept this up, he might slam her against the wall and make love to her, not caring that he was in his sister's condo with everyone looking on.

Nessa returned with four bags and handed them to him before facing Lily. "I'm so glad you were able to go out with us, Lily."

She spun to face Nessa and when she teetered, Birk steadied her. "Thank you for inviting me. It was an awesome day." She handed Nessa her glass.

"We'll have to do another girls' day when all this Toma stuff is over."

"Absolutely. I loved getting to know you and really appreciate how welcoming you all have been." Her words came out a bit slurred.

All four women hugged her goodbye, and Birk puffed out his chest, proud that his future mate got along so well with his family. And here he had worried for nothing.

He placed a hand on Lily's back. "Ready?"

"Yes."

"Did you have a good time?" he asked when they were halfway down the hall.

"I had an amazing time. Not only was it fun to shop and have makeovers, I learned so much about everyone, especially Kaleena's story about her incarceration and her eventual release."

At least she hadn't said the highlight was watching porn. "I've always admired Kaleena's strength. If I'd been in the same situation, I'm not sure if I'd have handled it as well."

Lily sighed. "She told me about the people unjustly locked up in the castle. Is there anything you can do about it?"

Birk tightened his hold around her waist. The last thing he ever wanted was to disappoint Lily, but right now he needed to ensure her safety. "My father and uncle are working on a plan. Declan and Finn will lend a hand as soon as this whole mess with Toma clears up."

She sagged against him, and he wasn't sure if it was because of the alcohol or because she wanted his warmth. "I hope you figure something out."

"I'm sure we will." He pressed the down button. "Enough of the sad talk. I want to know everything you did, though from the looks of it, I'd say you stopped in quite a few stores."

She faced him. "We did." She listed just a few. "You really like the new me?" she asked, her eyelids half closing.

"Like I said, I think you look amazing, though I loved the way you looked before too. I didn't say anything, because I didn't want to gush over you in front of Greer and Tory. Remember, they have no one to go home to."

"I hadn't thought of that."

"Just so you know, it took all of my control not to pin you against the wall and kiss you senseless like you wanted me to." *And strip you naked and then make love to you.*

Her eyes widened. "Like I still want you to?" He nodded. "You're right."

Birk chuckled. Once they arrived at his condo, he couldn't wait to taste her. Being away from Lily all day had him on the brink of despair.

As soon as they stepped inside his place, she faced him. "Can I try on a few things for you that I bought?"

Birk inwardly groaned. He'd never be able to see her in sexy clothes and not tear them off her. "If I can help you get out of them."

She laughed and held up her hands. "No, you have to behave and watch. Once you touch me, you know what will happen."

"Only too well."

Before he could snatch her into his arms and kiss her like he'd been wanting to from the moment he'd stepped into Nessa's place, Lily grabbed the shopping bags from his hands and ran into her room. He debated going after her, but she seemed really excited to show him what she'd purchased. Birk needed to put her joy over his needs.

While Lily changed, Birk paced. When she hadn't emerged after five minutes, he snagged a beer from the fridge to help settle him down. After the frustrating day he and the others had, he needed to relax. Halfway through the bottle, Lily opened the door and stepped out.

"Holy shit, you look fantastic!" He hadn't wanted her to think the outfit made the woman, but the high heels, short black skirt, along with the bright turquoise, low-cut fitted top made his cock so hard he had to adjust himself. Not to mention he glowed as bright as a neon sign.

She spun around. "Greer picked out most of the items."

"Remind me to give my sister a hug." He stepped toward her. "Did you buy any sexy underwear?"

She grinned. "Why yes I did."

"I hope you're going to let me unwrap my present now."

"I thought you'd never ask."

Lily was such a tease, and he loved it. "I asked before if I could strip you naked and you turned me down. I'm glad you've changed your mind this time," Birk said, his words coming out slow and deep.

She stepped close, kicked off her heels, and then ran a finger down his chest, stopping at the waistband of his jeans. "Hmm. How about I start here and we see where things lead? If I recall, you promised I could have some wicked fun with you the next time."

Lily had changed radically in the last few days, and he hoped it was because she accepted the idea of them being together—or else the alcohol had reduced her inhibitions.

"Did I say that?" Birk grinned.

"Yes."

"Fine, but I want you to know that I've had to work oh so hard to protect you."

She laughed. "Is that so?"

"Mmhmm. So how are you going to make it up to me?" As much as he wanted to take her clothes off and drive his hard cock into her, Lily deserved some tender loving, and he wanted to give her the lead. Birk would do all he could to relax and let her explore. This was her time, but it was going to be torture for sure—sweet and divine.

"By doing this." She undid the button on his jeans, causing anticipation and the strongest of yearnings to course through him. "I'm curious to know just how many ruby scales I can make glow."

"My dragon might emerge."

Lily wagged a finger at him. "You can't pull that trick on me anymore. I asked the girls whether or not they had ever experienced a loss of control and shifted."

"They're only women."

She shook her head. "They said men and women shifters are equal when it comes to desire and need."

He huffed out a laugh. "Nessa told you that, right?"

"Yes."

Birk knew when he was defeated. He stretched out his arms and kicked off his shoes. "Then go for it, but don't be surprised if I can't hold out and have to strip you naked, something doesn't get ruined."

Her jaw dropped. "You wouldn't."

"Not on purpose, but I am on edge right now. I've been away

from you all day and my dragon and I need you something fierce."

"I like your dragon."

"That so? How about showing him?"

Birk had no idea why he challenged her. One lick on his cock and he might partially shift. He probably should turn his hands into claws to prove to her that she could only seduce him up to a point.

Lily grinned, undid the zipper, and dragged down his pants. Removing them could be a bit tricky, so he helped. After she lifted off his shirt, he was finally standing in front of her naked, and the light from his scales cast a reddish glow on the wall.

She dragged the tip of her finger up the length of his cock, hard enough to feel but way too light to satisfy. Birk hissed.

Lily looked up. "Does that mean you like this?"

Damn woman would be the death of him. "I more than like it, but I suggest you hurry before I explode." He was right. It was definite torture.

She bent over, and then glanced up at him through her lashes. "Just a few licks."

Lily must be part seductress because the moment her mouth slid down his cock, his claws extended, and he struggled with his usual iron control.

As much as Birk wanted to grab hold and direct her to take his cock deep, he wouldn't for fear of hurting her. Instead, he gently gathered her hair and held it in a makeshift ponytail while he ran his other hand down the side of her face and neck. He would let her find her own pace—for now anyway.

Lily grabbed the bottom half of his shaft and then sucked on the rest of his dick. He squeezed his eyes shut to focus on keeping control, but her moans and soft mewling caused him to lose it. The last thing he'd planned on was to let go, but his climax had snuck up on him too fast to stop. As he pumped his seed into her mouth, Lily held him tighter, exciting him further.

Once he finished, he slipped out of her hold. "I'm really sorry," he said. "I swear that's never happened to me before."

Lily swallowed, looked up at him, and then grinned. "I'll take that as a compliment. I have to say, from the way you were swaying, moaning, and flashing, you enjoyed it."

"Damn right, I did." He gathered her in his arms and held her tight, her flowery scent overwhelming his senses. "How about we head into the bedroom where you can model for me whatever else you bought?"

Lily giggled. "You just want to see me undress."

"Hell yes, I do! Let's go, I'm up for an X-rated fashion show!" Birk slapped her on the ass as she squealed and ran ahead to the bedroom.

TRYING ON ALL of her new outfits for Birk last night had been such a high. Not only did his eyes glow and his hands turn into claws twice, he ended up begging her for sex. Only when Lily had shown him every outfit and teased him mercilessly did she give in. Truth be told, seeing him so desperate soothed all the hurt she'd endured from assholes like Nelor Dobbins.

After making love twice, they snuggled in bed where Birk fell asleep right away. As tired as she was—and as satisfied—Lily couldn't take her mind off of those poor souls who were trapped inside the castle. Since the Royals were the highest authority in Avonbelle, it wasn't as if they'd listen if she went there to complain about the injustice. Her luck, they'd toss her into the cell right alongside the others.

"Lily?" a deep voice said, rousing her.

Birk's voice finally reached her brain, and she bolted upright. "Is something wrong?" She glanced around, noticing that the once dark room was now filled with light. "What time is it?"

He chuckled. "It's only ten, but I ordered in some breakfast, and it just arrived."

She hadn't remembered falling asleep, but apparently she had.

Lily tossed back the blanket, placed her feet on the floor, and then stretched. "I'll be right there."

"I'll pour the coffee."

After she dressed, washed her face, and brushed her teeth, she padded out to the living room. On the dining room table Birk claimed he rarely used, sat two bags of food from Arnolds that smelled divine. "I love their food."

"Me too." He carried over two steaming cups of coffee, motioning her to sit down. "What would you like to do today?" he asked.

When she'd had trouble sleeping, she'd given some thought what she wanted to do today. "What do you say we take a trip to the eternal flame?"

His forehead wrinkled. "Why would you want to go there? It's a long journey."

"It is only long if we drive."

"Are you saying you want to experience the Birk Express Flight?"

She laughed. "At some point in my life I suspect something will come up that requires a speedy trip. I might as well see if I'm afraid of flying without a seatbelt."

He sipped his steaming drink. "I would be delighted to give it a try, but if it scares you, we can always drive there."

"That would take too long. Let's hope I'm okay with being dangled from long claws high in the air. Kyle said that when Nessa first carried him, he felt safe."

"I promise you'll feel safe too. I've never dropped anyone."

"I'm glad." Lily opened up her bag of food and sighed when she saw the egg and cheese croissant. "You bought my favorite. Thank you."

Birk smiled and pulled out the contents of his bag. "Why do you want to visit the eternal flame?"

Lily believed in total honesty. "I'm hoping to run into your fairy lady."

"She's hardly my lady. You are."

Lily waved a hand. "You know what I mean—the lady who told

you I was in trouble with Toma's associates. Maybe she's learned something new."

"She might have."

"I also want to see if this magical person knows anything about the people held captive in the castle."

"Ah, so this is your real reason for wanting to go."

"Maybe, but I can't help it," she said. "There's something so tragic about their plight. I know that you and your family are still working on a rescue plan, but since Kaleena's been free for quite some time now, it could be a bit longer before your family comes up with something."

Birk reached out and grabbed her hand. "You have the most beautiful heart, Lily Harper."

Heat raced up her face at the compliment. "Thank you."

"How about we finish eating, and then I'll take you on a trial flight?"

She smiled, and her love for Birk bloomed. "Up, up, and away we go."

Chapter Thirteen

B IRK STEPPED BACK about fifteen feet from Lily in order to have enough room to shift. Shielding her eyes from the bright sun, she waited for him to transform. Not that Lily knew much about flying, but the minimal winds seemed like ideal conditions. Later she'd ask him if the rain and gusty conditions made flight more difficult even though his scales were waterproof.

"I'm going to shift now," Birk warned. "I am rather large in my dragon form, so please don't freak out."

"I've seen a dragon before. They've been flying overhead my whole life," Lily said.

"Good. Do you remember what to do if you become scared and want me to land?"

She sighed. They'd been over this several times. "Yes. One squeeze on your talon means slow down or level off, and two squeezes mean I'm done and want you to land right away."

He grinned. "You got it. Are you ready?"

"As I'll ever be."

Determined not to be afraid, Lily pictured the eternal flame and the tiny blonde woman in the hopes of finding answers. Nessa had told her how incredible and helpful Fay had been to her and Kyle. While the woman's message had been rather cryptic, it had provided just enough information for Nessa to figure out who was after them.

Wind swooshed across Lily's face. One minute, Birk was human, and the next, he was this soaring mass of black and ruby scales. Holy shit! He was huge—bigger than Kyle in fact. She couldn't imagine growing that large in mere seconds. It had to hurt.

Birk reached out slowly, and Lily grabbed hold of his talon. They'd discussed whether she wanted to be cradled against his chest or face downward in order to watch the landscape pass by.

For her trial run, she chose to face upward. Birk lifted her up, but before she was mentally ready, he burst upward. Wind swept her hair from her face, and the pressure from the change in gravity caused her to grip his talons harder and her heart to shoot to her throat. It was almost like the first time she'd gone downhill on a rollercoaster. Everything in her body freaked out for a bit.

Lily could almost hear Birk's comforting words about how he'd never dropped anyone, and that helped her relax—somewhat. Concentrating on his chest, she forced herself to breathe evenly. Thankfully, heat from his body took away the chill from being this high up.

For the next few minutes, Birk flew parallel to the ground, and Lily eventually released her death grip—that was until he headed downward again. She swore she was falling. Tapping his talon twice was useless since he was headed to the ground anyway.

Trying to be brave, she thought about the lovemaking from last night and the look in Birk's eyes when she'd taken off her red lace push-up bra. She loved how his irises had changed colors several times. Usually when he was excited, they were pure turquoise, but this time swirls of green and amber had skidded across the surface.

Birk set her down before she realized he'd landed. A bit disoriented, she clasped his claw for a moment before letting go. He needed to shift back, so she stepped away from him. Seconds later, he was human again.

"How was it?" He leaned forward, his body language implying he was anxious.

"Good. It was a bit nerve wracking at first, but when I let my mind wander to other things, I was fine."

"Does that mean you're ready for your hour-long trip? I want to make sure my grip wasn't too tight."

He was the most thoughtful man. "No, it was perfect."

He grinned. "Face up or face down this time?"

Lily was brave but not that brave. "Face up going there. I might change my mind for the return trip."

Birk stepped closer. "I'd kiss you right now, but if I start…"

She laughed. "You won't be able to stop. I know."

Probably because he didn't trust his dragon, Birk moved back and then shifted once more. This time when he swooped her up and took off, Lily was far more comfortable with the increase in speed.

After several minutes of being in the air, she looked over her shoulder at the ground below, and to her delight the view didn't disorient her. In fact, from this high up, the landscape was spectacular. A girl could get used to this mode of transportation.

Sooner than she thought possible, Birk landed and then shifted once more. It was hard to believe an hour had passed.

He rushed up to her. "Are you okay?"

"Yes, why wouldn't I be? I didn't squirm or cry out, did I?"

His shoulders sagged. "No. Did you enjoy the flight?"

She loved his hopeful expression. "Totally."

"I can't tell you how relieved I am."

She rubbed his arm. "Me too."

"We'll have to walk a bit before we reach the flame. I couldn't fly any closer because of all the trees."

"I figured."

The path was flat and easy to navigate. Nessa had said she and Kyle had spotted no one on the trail, but this time two couples, one with two teenagers in tow, passed them. When she and Birk arrived at the sacred spot, Lily was a little disappointed at the less than spectacular fountain. Four pipes protruded from the mountain face, each with water flowing out of them that fed a small pool. In front, and slightly to the side, was a large cement bowl that contained the eternal flame.

While the size of the flame was impressive, there wasn't a fairy or a blonde woman around anywhere, and there weren't any fireflies either—something else Birk had said he'd seen the last time he'd visited.

He led her to the fountain. "The last time I made a wish, Fay appeared. Maybe that's how we contact her."

"It would be fun to make a wish anyway."

Birk handed her a coin. "Close your eyes, make a wish, and then toss in the coin."

With the metal pressed against her palm, Lily faced the fountain and tried to picture those lost souls trapped in the jail. *I hope Birk and his family can find a way to save them.*

Once she mentally spoke her desire, she opened her eyes and tossed in the coin. There were several other different denominations at the bottom of the pool. She spun around and looked deep into the forest, waiting for Fay to arrive.

"Where is she?" Lily asked.

He shrugged. "Maybe she has the day off."

That was lame. "I doubt that. She appeared for Kyle and Nessa."

Birk placed a hand on the small of her back. "Let's read the inscription on the flame. I didn't get a chance to look at it the last time."

For the next few minutes they read about the four provinces and their pledge to remain allies. "Do you think the provinces decided to unite because they believed Earth or Cargonia would challenge them?" she asked.

"I don't know. Maybe if we run into Fay again, we can ask her."

All of a sudden, a strange buzzing sound came from down the pathway. They both turned at once and watched a swarm of pinpoint lights come toward them. Birk stepped slightly in front of Lily. A moment later, the individual pinpricks grouped together and transformed into a small, blonde woman.

A beautiful creature, full of light herself, smiled and held out her hand to Birk. "Nice to see you again." She faced Lily. "And this must be your mate."

"Yes, this is Lily Harper." Birk wrapped an arm around Lily's waist.

"Nice to meet you Lily—I'm Fay Forrester. I trust Birk has been keeping you safe?" Fay asked as sweet as could be.

Lily's lips wouldn't move. She'd never seen anyone like Fay before.

"I'm trying to," Birk said. "We came because Lily was hoping to meet you."

Finally, her breath returned to her lungs. "Yes. We were curious if you learned anything more about the men who want to harm me."

Fay shook her head. "Information comes to me in waves. It's not like I have Internet service here and can type in my question."

Her comical answer relaxed Lily. "I understand. I do have one more thing to ask, and it doesn't require that kind of knowledge."

Fay's eyes lit up. "I'll be happy to help if I can."

"There are people—white lighters we believe—who are trapped in the basement of the Royal castle. They are being held in order for the Royals to steal their magic." Lily told her about Kaleena and Finn's remarkable rescue.

"I did hear about that. It was tragic."

That was all she could say? "Is there anything Birk and his family can do to save them?" *Or anything you can do?*

"You sound very passionate about them. Do you know any of them personally?"

"No, but I can imagine what it would be like being trapped—especially if I did nothing wrong. I'm not a shifter, and I have no power, but if I did, and someone wanted to mess with it, I'd be terrified and quite upset."

"I see." Fay turned around and strolled toward the forest. She stopped and then spun back. "I might have a solution."

Lily's pulse soared. "What's that?"

"How would you like to save them?"

Laughter burst out of her. "Me? Not only is the underground part of the castle a maze, I have no powers."

"What if you did?"

Lily didn't know how to answer.

Fay moved closer. "What if I told you that I could give you the power of invisibility one time? And that whatever you touched would become invisible too? That way, you could sweep in, unlock the cells, and lead the prisoners out."

Had Birk not had his arm around her waist, she might have collapsed. "For real?" She looked up at him to see his reaction.

"If someone bumped into her, would they know she was there?" Birk asked, his voice coming out hard.

"Yes, but in the time it took this person to react, Lily could move out of harm's way."

Her mind spun. Finding the prisoners was a daunting enough task, let alone freeing them, but if she were invisible, it might be possible.

"When would this spell start?" Birk asked, his voice lower.

Fay lifted something from her pocket. It was an amulet of some sort, and she handed it to Lily. "It's not a spell in the traditional sense. If you place this over your heart and say the words: *pure of soul, kind of heart, I shall be free to do my part*, the power of invisibility will begin."

Birk slid one of Lily's hands into his.

The chant sounded rather hokey to her, but she had nothing to lose. "Once I'm invisible, how do I change back to being seen again?"

"To go from invisible to visible, place the stone over your heart once more and repeat the chant. After you use the amulet, the next time you return, give it to me so I can offer it to someone else."

"Of course." Her heart pounded as she squeezed the metal piece tightly in her palm. She looked up at Birk. "What do you think?"

He let go of her hand and cupped her face. "It's up to you, baby, but I think we can come up with a plan to make this work, if that's what you want. Since it only works once, maybe you want to use it if you are ever captured by Toma's men."

Lily shook her head. "No, I have you to protect me. I want to do some good with my new power."

Fay smiled. "Then enjoy your day of being a rescuer."

Lily didn't know how to thank her. "May I hug you?"

Fay spread her arms. "All creatures need to be appreciated."

The embrace that followed was warm and wonderful. "Thank you," Lily said.

"My pleasure. Now, if you two are worried about being safe, there is a cabin not far from here where you can relax. The fireflies will make sure nothing happens to you. We fairies use it all the time."

Heat swamped her. "It is your cabin?" Lily blurted.

"For today, it's yours."

It didn't seem as if Fay was going to give out any more information. "I don't know what to say."

Fay laughed. "No need to say anything. Enjoy the natural beauty of our forest here. I have no doubt you have a few ideas of your own on how to spend the rest of your day at the cabin together."

Lily understood very little, but she was thrilled. "Thank you for everything, Fay!"

As quickly as she appeared, the fairy turned into a small winged creature and then disappeared into pinpricks of light.

"I've never seen anything like that before," Lily said with total awe.

"I hadn't either. Ready to find this cabin?" Birk asked.

"You bet. Besides, the walk will give me some time to come to grips with what just happened. I can't believe I saw a fairy appear and disappear into what looked like fireflies. And then I learned I could appear and disappear at will—at least one time. It's overwhelming."

"I imagine it would be."

"Let's not forget, I had my first ever dragon flight today too. I'll be marking this day on my calendar."

Birk stroked her arm. "I've interacted with the Four Sisters of Fate on several occasions, so being able to give you this kind of ability shouldn't surprise me, but it does. As for this being a red-letter day, I'm hoping to make it even more memorable." He winked.

Her heart nearly jumped out of her body from the sheer joy racing through her. Lily stuck her hand in her pocket and rubbed her thumb over the surface of the amulet to make sure she still had it.

Less than fifteen minutes later, they arrived at an adorable white wooden cottage. It had green shutters and a porch with pink and green rocking chairs on it.

"Let's look inside," Birk said. "I bet we can think of something *fun* to do."

Lily laughed. "Do you think of anything besides sex?"

His mouth opened. "How can you ask me that? I think about your safety, your comfort, if you're happy, and—"

She smiled and held up a hand. "I was only teasing you. Come on."

Chapter Fourteen

"DO YOU THINK we really are safe here?" Lily asked. "I mean—can fireflies really keep us safe?"

"I believe they can. This forest is full of magic." Birk had been brought up to respect that. So what if he'd been skeptical at first? "Even if the fireflies aren't able to ward off any evil, I can protect you." He drew her near and then hugged her. Lily's scent tantalized him, and a wave of need descended. "I want you, Lily."

"I want you too."

Lily had been through so much today, and her acceptance of the changes made him love her even more. His lips descended, and when she opened her mouth to receive him, all thoughts of taking their love making experience slow, disappeared.

She reached for the button on his pants first. "I need you naked," she said after breaking the kiss.

He laughed. "I thought that was my line."

With a speed he couldn't believe, they both kicked off their shoes. Birk quickly unbuttoned her shirt and then started on her pants while she undid the zipper on his jeans and tugged on them. When she dropped to her knees to take them off, he let go of her pants before he had the chance to remove them.

Against his will, his claws extended. *Stop it*, he said to his dragon. They slowly transformed into hands again. "Sorry. My dragon is having a hard time behaving. He wants you too much—as do I."

Lily stood. "I remember what happened the last time your dragon was in need, and I sucked on your dick."

"It exploded, which should be a lesson to you." Birk stepped back and ditched his pants, briefs, and shirt.

Lily stood there, light filling her eyes. "I never get tired of seeing you naked."

"Can I finish undressing you?"

"If you're fast."

Oh, I'll be fast all right. I couldn't go slowly if I wanted to. "I'll try not to destroy anything. We don't want to walk through the woods with torn clothes."

Lily's eyes widened. She slipped off her unbuttoned shirt, un-hooked her bra, and tossed it on the counter. The mere sight of her naked breasts had Birk's hormones going crazy.

Lily shoved her pants down. Birk then knelt in front of her and dragged her pink panties along with her jeans the rest of the way. His chest expanded and contracted too rapidly, and his fingers itched to touch her intimately.

She held onto the counter and stepped out of the rest of her clothes. Birk stood and lifted her up onto the counter.

Her eyes opened wide again. "Holy crap, that is cold."

"Oh, shit. I'm sorry." The Earth saying of haste makes waste sure applied here. Birk tossed his jeans on the counter. "Sit on these."

Once she was on them, Lily smiled. "Much better."

With nothing else to get in their way, Birk spread her legs. He then picked up his shirt, folded it in half, and placed it behind her so she didn't hurt her elbows. "Lean back."

Ready for his feast, he slipped two fingers into her pussy and wiggled them around, searching for that perfect spot that made her scream in ecstasy. Lily sat up and grabbed his shoulders, scratching his skin in the process. His scales glowed, and no doubt his eyes had turned a different shade.

"Kiss me, Birk."

Cupping the back of her head, Birk delved into her mouth. With his fingers still buried deep inside her, he kept working that sweet spot while his thumb flicked her clit. His dragon clawed at his insides as his balls tightened.

Lily broke the kiss, dropped her head back, and let out a yell, her climax overtaking her. A moment later, she was back on her elbows, her chest heaving. "That was amazing."

Birk smiled and withdrew his fingers. "I have something bigger if you want?"

She chuckled. "I have something bigger for you to put your mouth on too." She sat up and lifted her breasts. It was like she was waving a red cape at a bull.

"Fuck me. I don't know where to start. I want it all."

As if she'd placed a huge feast in front of him, Birk sucked on one breast while he kneaded the other. Sparks of lust pummeled his body, and his cock grew harder than the stone counter. With each lick, his need grew. After he switched to the other breast, he dropped between her legs and swiped his tongue across her opening.

She shrieked with pleasure.

Mate, mate, his dragon urged.

As much as Birk wanted to claim her as his own right then, he needed to wait. She wasn't ready yet.

Soon though.

"Birk, please, I have to have you."

He stood, slid her off the counter, turned her around, and placed her hands on the stone top. When he widened her legs with his, he noticed his cum had leaked out.

Don't fail me now, dragon.

Then hurry.

LILY WAS SO on edge. Her pussy was aching for Birk's cock. She gripped the counter hard and arched her back, hoping he was so excited that he wouldn't notice her ugly, scarred back. Even though Birk told her it didn't bother him, she still doubted him. He was just being kind because who wouldn't be put off by such ugliness?

But when Birk placed his cheek on her back and pressed his hard shaft against her opening, all doubt evaporated, and love bloomed. Her body sizzled with delight. Instead of plunging into her though, he cupped her breasts and nibbled on her ear. What was he waiting for? An invitation?

"I love the feel of these," he said as he squeezed her nipples. They stiffened and heat raced between her thighs.

"I love when you touch them." The breath was knocked from her lungs from the excitement soaring through her veins, causing her words to come out as a whisper.

Birk chuckled. "Then I'll have to touch them often."

He pressed on the tips, sending erotic lust straight to her core, and every twist and turn made her body yearn for more. Lily leaned her hips back to signal she was ready. It must have been what he was waiting for, because he lowered his hands to her waist and drove into her.

Oh, glory. Cascading waves of pure bliss slammed into her hard, and she lifted her head to suck in more oxygen. He slipped out and then tunneled straight back in again, causing her pussy to spasm around his cock. Her flesh quivered. Her heart pounded. Joy blasted her.

She reached behind her and grabbed his right hip, thrilling at the way his muscles bunched with each thrust. Birk lowered his lips to her neck, and for a moment Lily thought this would be the moment when he sank his teeth into her and made her his own. As much as she wanted to be one with him, she needed more time.

Lily must have stiffened because Birk moved on, kissing his way downward until his mouth was pressed against her shoulder.

"Lily, you have no idea what you do to me." His gravelly voice nearly undid her.

"I wish you could be me for one moment to understand what I'm feeling."

Birk nuzzled his face against her neck again and groaned as he plowed into her. She sucked in deep breaths as her climax built. When he lowered a hand between her legs and pressed on her clit, her resolve collapsed. A gigantic orgasm swept in, taking her as high as when Birk had flown her above the realm.

When he buried himself deep inside her, his hot seed filled her. At that moment, they were one.

She was overwhelmed. Satisfied. And reeling. Never in a million years would she have believed a dragon shifter could bring her such joy. But he had. Birk. Her Birk. Wow.

Lily folded her arms on the counter and dropped her forehead on her wrists, her back heaving from the experience.

His heavy breath rolled over her ear as he whispered, "You are so amazing."

She would have responded had her brain been able to form the words. All she could do was nod. Lily thought he would pull out, but instead he nibbled on her ear again and his hard cock slowly eased out and then slid back in again.

"I can't get enough of you," he said.

Ribbons of desire wrapped around her body and ruby red flashes of light made it past her closed lids. She wanted to tell him she wanted him again, but Lily wasn't good at expressing herself, so she showed him. Grabbing his hand, she slid it between her legs.

The smart man figured out what she wanted before she did. Birk gently bit her ear and then dragged his lips to her cheek as his thumb pressed on her clit again. How she could be so excited three times in a row she didn't know, but every one of his touches made her more urgent than the last.

"Yes," she managed to say. "That's it."

Once his already slick cock reached the end of her channel, her brain ceased to function. Sparks lit up every cell, and it was as if he were transporting her to a different realm. One hand continued to lovingly press and twirl her clit while the other excited her breasts.

"I need you more than life, Lily."

She let his words bathe her in acceptance, and her love bloomed. Unable to control her body, she pressed her hips back. That did it. Birk grunted, increased the pressure on her nipples and thrust into her hard.

Soaring high once more, she let go and went on the wild ride with him. Colors swam in front of her and endorphins filled her veins. Time seemed to stand still. As if this was going to be the last time they'd ever have the chance to make love, their sweaty bodies glided easily over one another. Their lovemaking was deliciously fast and furious.

His lips pressed against her head, and he inhaled deeply. The groan that followed and the hard pinch to her nipples was the final push to yet another realm-shattering climax.

She yelled out, her body stiffening from the intensity of the pleasure of his cock detonating. Her face pressed against his rough wadded up jeans, her body sagged. Even Birk seemed frozen to the spot. She stayed cocooned in his arms for a long time before he withdrew.

"Jeez, Lily. You will be the death of me. That was incredible," he said as he padded over to a drawer and opened it. The water ran, and when he returned, he turned her around and wiped her clean.

"I'm spent," she said.

Once Birk washed, and then tossed the wet cloth back into the sink, he lifted her into his arms. "Are you ready to head out of the forest?"

Was he kidding? She draped her arms around his neck and sagged against him. "Give me a minute to recuperate."

Birk nuzzled her neck. "Take as long as you need. I love holding you."

Chapter Fifteen

A S BIRK AND Lily headed back to the clearing at the edge of the forest, she was highly animated about saving the prisoners. Birk was not. "Do you have a plan in mind?" he asked.

"Not really, but according to Kaleena, Finn recorded the castle maze that leads to the cells. I'll study it until it's burned into my memory. Then I'll ask for the prison cell keys Finn took from the castle, find my way there, and free the prisoners."

There was so much more than simple logistics, but he didn't want to argue with her now. "For starters, we have to make sure the people there are unjustifiably imprisoned."

"Kaleena said she met—"

He held up a hand. "Kaleena doesn't really know. It's been a while since she was held captive. The white lighters might have been turned already. It's also possible some of them are killers."

Lily kicked a clump of dirt. "I hadn't thought of that."

Birk hated seeing her dejected, so he wrapped an arm around her shoulder. "We'll sit down with the other Guardians and work out a solid plan. Don't worry, we will figure something out." Something that would involve a certain set of sisters. "Before we even think of letting you head into the castle, I want to have Camden see if he can embed a tracking device in your ring. I couldn't live with myself if anything went wrong. A worst-case scenario would be if you became visible while freeing the prisoners and are caught. At least then I could find you if they take you someplace else."

She hugged his arm. "That's a wonderful idea, but let's hope it won't come to that. Fay never mentioned anything about me losing my invisibility shield though."

"True, but I'm all about contingencies."

THE FLIGHT BACK to town wasn't nearly as scary as her first flight, possibly because Lily's mind alternated between the incredible sex she and Birk had in the cottage, and the realization she now possessed some magic—or would possess some magic once she placed the amulet Fay had given her over her heart and repeated a chant.

They were now seated at a large conference table in the SinCas building.

"Sugar or milk?" Birk asked as he set a cup of coffee in front of her.

"After being my bodyguard all that time, you don't remember I take it black?"

He stabbed a hand through his hair. "Sorry. I forgot. The thought of something going wrong with this crazy operation has short-circuited my brain."

She reached out and grabbed his hand. "What can go wrong? No one will be able to see me."

"You know how we can cloak ourselves when we fly?"

He'd demonstrated his ability to her when they were in the air. "Yes."

"Sometimes even that goes haywire. Stress can distract us and cause our shield to disappear. Even just being invisible for too long can sometimes make us lose it. What if that happens to you?"

"Fay would have warned us." She held up a hand. "But if it does happen, I'll just tell them I'm lost."

He raised his brows. "Lost inside a dungeon? They won't buy it."

"They don't have any use for me. I'm not a white lighter, and I'm not a shifter. They would be able to sense it."

"That may be true, but I still don't like it."

The door to the boardroom opened, and Finn, Kaleena, and

Nessa entered. Lily was a little disappointed Kyle wasn't with them. A few more thumps sounded on the roof above them, and she glanced upward.

"It's probably Declan, Thane, or Dad. Hell, it could be any of them," Birk said with confidence.

She nodded, remembering the sound Birk made when he landed. While those three fixed a drink, Declan, Mr. Sinclair, and Mr. Caspian barreled in. Birk's dad nodded at her. "Nice to see you again, Lily."

"You too." He'd come to the underground safe house from time to time to speak with his son when Birk was doing her bodyguard duty.

After everyone grabbed their drink of choice and a snack, they crowded around the table. Birk began by detailing what Fay Forrester had told them. "Show them the amulet, hon."

She pulled the round piece of metal from her pocket and placed it on the table. Everyone looked, but no one picked it up.

Nessa placed something on the table and slid it to Lily. "This is the camera feed Finn took. Study it thoroughly. I'm hoping it will help you figure out how to reach the cells."

"I can help with that," Finn said. "If I look at the images again, I should be able to draw a fairly good diagram for you too."

Lily smiled. "That would be great."

The door opened again and Kyle rushed in. "Sorry, I'm late. Work demanded my attention." He took the seat between Nessa and Lily and then leaned over. "What's this I heard about you becoming temporarily invisible?"

She went through what Fay had told her and then pointed to the amulet.

Kyle looked over at Nessa. "Remember, my former assistant had that talent—except he could do it whenever he wanted. Trust me, when Landry snuck up on me, I didn't hear a thing."

"I hope I'm just as quiet," Lily said.

"Birk, do you have a plan?" his dad asked, turning everyone's attention to him.

"Only that I'll ask Camden to embed a tracking device into Lily's ring."

"Smart thinking."

"Secondly, I'd like to contact the Four Sisters to see if they can learn which of the captives should be saved," Birk said.

Lily certainly didn't want to go on a dangerous mission only to find out she'd freed bad people. She faced Birk. "Do you believe the sisters really can find out?"

"We can only hope." Birk clasped her hand and gave it a light squeeze. He faced the group. "Let's pretend Lily can find her way to the jail cells. Then what? What if the locks have been changed since Finn took the keys?"

Lily's stomach churned. The number of unknowns was mounting.

"Since we have the keys, I'll create a keyhole to match it that Lily can practice on. If they did rekey it, I can teach Lily how to pick the lock," Thane said.

Her fingers trembled just thinking about trying to do something like that under pressure. "What if I can't do it? Isn't there some other way?" She looked around the room.

"Perhaps one of the sisters will know of something," Mr. Sinclair said.

For the next few hours, they discussed strategies about timing, routes, escape plans, and emergency protocols. During that time, Finn volunteered to deliver Lily's ring to Camden in the hope he could hide something inside the ring that would allow Birk to keep track of her.

Just before the group broke, Camden stepped into the room. "I have Lily's ring, and I created something that might solve the unlocking issue Finn told me about. Mind you, it won't work on any of our sophisticated locks, but old metal ones are susceptible to vibrations." He handed her the ring, along with a small box. Inside it contained something that looked like a lock pick.

"This will unlock the doors?" she asked, twisting the piece of metal in her hands.

"All you have to do is put this pick into the lock, turn on the device, and then slowly rotate the dial clockwise. When you hear a clicking sound, twist the key hard to open the door."

"Really?"

"Come to the lab afterward, and I'll let you try it on a lock similar to the ones in the castle cellar."

"I'm impressed," Thane said.

Camden grinned. "Being a geek has its benefits."

He looked nothing like a geek, what with his black hair, fit physique, and a smile that would melt most women's panties. These families had good genes, but Birk was the only one who held her heart.

Lily was so excited at this new twist. This made the possibility of success that much greater. "Thank you so much."

Birk's father stood. "I still would like the sisters' advice on who to save. Their pottery shop should be closed right about now, so we'll have privacy. Birk, why don't the three of us head on over there and see what we can find out."

"Sounds good." Birk looked around. "I'll be in touch later to let you know when we plan to do this escape. We'll need everyone's help with this. If anything goes wrong, I want to be able to storm the castle."

He was overreacting, but that was her Birk. She reached up and grabbed his hand. "I'll be fine."

"I hope so, but we always plan for something to go wrong. It's better to be prepared than taken by surprise."

She could understand that.

Almost everyone headed up to the rooftop. Seeing so many people transform into dragons mesmerized her.

Kyle hugged her. "I'm so proud of you."

"Why? Because I want to save some people?"

"I am proud of you for that, but I was talking about how you've been able to let go of your fear of dragons. You seem happy. For that I'm proud of you."

"Thank you." Since Birk was standing in front of her, she was a little embarrassed to say it had been all Birk's doing. It was stupid not to tell him how much he meant to her, but she wasn't ready to say those three little words when he hadn't said them first.

"Take care, sis."

The others shifted and took off.

Birk faced her. "Face up or face down?" Then he wiggled his eyebrows at her.

Lily laughed and rolled her eyes at him. She understood Birk was only trying to help keep things lighthearted and fun for her. He always seemed to put her first.

The first two times, she'd opted for not looking at the ground. Since this trip was short, she decided that if she was too afraid to look this time she had no right to assume she'd have it together enough to sneak into a castle and save a bunch of prisoners. "Face down."

Birk smiled and her heart melted. "That's my girl."

The takeoff was hairy, but once they passed a few familiar landmarks, Lily began to relax. She trusted Birk completely, and by the time they reached their destination, she was actually enjoying the ride.

Seeing the ground race toward her was a bit heart pounding, but the landing was smooth. Birk set her down and then shifted. His dad was already inside talking with three women. "Ready?" Birk asked as he held out a hand.

"Yes." A lot rode on the magical women she'd heard so much about. Between altering Finn's face, to disguising Nessa's dragon shifter signature, and then creating her protection ring, these women seemed to be able to do anything they wished.

With a hand on her back, Birk led her inside the store that smelled of cinnamon and lemon. It was as if the women had just polished all of the pots. While the display shelves were simple, the variety of pottery was amazing. They not only had the usual bowls, cups, and plates, but there were figurines, outdoor wall-hangings, and interesting masks. Some of Lily's friends had mentioned the store before, but she'd never been there.

"This is Poppy, Acacia, and Primrose," Birk's dad said, pointing to them in turn.

Lily shook each of their hands. "Nice to meet you."

For three such powerful women, Lily somehow expected them to be much older. While none of them wore make-up, they were pretty in their own way. Their hair was either plaited, in a ponytail, or in a bun, but all three wore dark pants and a colorful T-shirt.

"Show them your amulet," Birk said.

Carefully, Lily stuck her hand in her pocket, lifted it out, and held open her palm. "If I touch it to my chest and say *pure of soul, kind of heart, I shall be free to do my part*, I'll become invisible."

Poppy's eyes widened. "It wouldn't be the end of the world if you became invisible now. We do it all the time."

Birk's dad must not have explained the constraints. "I can only exercise the power once."

Poppy nodded. "Oh, I see. Then you need to choose wisely."

Laird Caspian explained about the plan to save those held prisoner by the Royals. "When Kaleena was there, there were about three or four others, some of whom were white lighters. By now, they could have been turned. Is there any way you can find out?"

The three women looked at each other and then back at them. "We really shouldn't interfere."

Birk stepped forward. "It's not like we're asking you to free them. Just tell us how many have been unjustly imprisoned and haven't been turned by the dark lighters."

Once more they faced each other, but this time they said nothing. Lily had to assume they were able to communicate telepathically like Kyle and Nessa could.

Poppy swiveled toward them. "The three of us will go. We agree that it would not be good if a dark lighter escaped by mistake.

Helping to aid you in freeing the innocent will only help in Fate's plan for the future, not interfere with it."

Relief swamped Lily. She rushed over to Poppy and hugged her. "Thank you so much."

"You're welcome. We're happy you want to help. That's mighty noble for a human."

If she played her cards right, she wouldn't be human for long.

"When can you find out?" Lily was anxious to finalize the plan before she lost her courage.

"Now."

With that the three women disappeared. Lily spun around to face Birk who had a knowing look on his face. "How can they do that?"

"It's magic."

Laird moved toward them. "No one knows what they are capable of. We're always thrilled when they are willing to help us."

Before she could respond, the three women reappeared, jump starting Lily's pulse.

Poppy smiled. "There are five prisoners, but only three are worthy."

Lily wouldn't ask how they'd figured all of that out in seconds. "Which three? I'll need descriptions."

Primrose stepped forward and held up a cell phone. "I took pictures of them. I'll send the photos to you."

This was too good to be true. "What did they say?"

The women looked at each other. "Say? Why, nothing. No one saw us, trust me."

Only now did she remember when she was invisible, if she touched something, it would become invisible too. "Of course." Lily told her where to send the pictures.

Laird and Birk thanked the ladies and escorted Lily out. Her mind spun. "I can't believe people can disappear like that."

"Why is that? You saw Fay do it."

Lily looked up at him, trying to recreate that image in her mind.

"True, but she started out as points of light."

Birk smiled and shook his head. "Ready for your ride?"

"Yes."

She found each time she went in the air with Birk was a bit easier. In fact, Lily loved being in Birk's arms—or rather his gentle claws. The trip to the SinCas building lasted only a few minutes, but the view was awesome. The three of them landed and the two men shifted.

Birk's dad faced them. "When do you think you will be ready, Lily?"

"As soon as I memorize the path. I might have to ask Finn to help."

He nodded. "Let us know. Now that we have a firm plan and know the innocents are still there and haven't been turned to dark lighters yet, we don't want to delay."

"I'll get right on this. Luckily, I have no cases at work, and I have some personal days I can use. Once again, thank you for everything."

"Our pleasure. Now get some rest, Lily. No matter how well we plan things, the stress can mess with your mind."

She nodded. Birk slipped an arm around her waist. "Up for some dinner?"

"I really need to study this video. Your dad is right. Time is critical."

"What about Grub Hub delivery?"

"Perfect."

Chapter Sixteen

A
FTER TWO STRAIGHT days of studying and receiving quite a lot of help from Finn, Lily was as ready for this mission as she would ever be. Alea had been awesome when Lily called and asked to use her personal days. She told Lily that she had everything covered and not to worry about a thing.

"You good?" Birk asked.

As much as Lily wanted to say no, she'd committed to this. "Yes."

He escorted her out of his condo and toward the elevator. "Remember, not only will I be nearby, your brother, Nessa, and the rest of the group will be too. You've got this."

"What if I get lost?" She patted her pocket to make sure she had the magical amulet, along with the piece of paper on which Finn had drawn a detailed map of the maze.

Birk squeezed her waist. "You've repeated the directions to me so many times, you can't get lost. The whole idea that no one can see you should keep you calm."

Unless some guard came toward her and she freaked. "I know. I think the biggest risk will be when I'm leading the prisoners out. What if one of them forgets and lets go of a hand?"

He pushed the elevator button. "You worry too much."

She didn't know how Birk remained so calm. He'd spent hours trying to talk her out of doing this. In the end, she'd won, though it wouldn't be called winning if she landed in a cell.

Once on the rooftop of his building, Birk faced her. "You have the amulet that Fay gave you, right?"

She couldn't help but roll her eyes. "Yes." Just to be sure she stuck her hand in her pocket again, pulled it out, and waved it at him.

Birk smiled, but the joy didn't reach his eyes. He was worried. Damn. "Let's do this."

He shifted before she could ask him if he thought this whole escape plan was stupid. When he reached out his claw, she climbed into her usual resting place.

As much as Lily tried to slow her heartbeat, she failed, and it wasn't because of flying. It was from all the warnings Birk had thrown at her last night.

A few minutes later, the castle appeared in the distance. Instead of taking her to the entrance, Birk landed quite far from it. Once he shifted, many of the Guardians emerged from the woods.

Kaleena rushed up to her. "You're doing a brave thing, Lily. Fate did a good job pairing you with my cousin."

Birk had told her she was brave too. To her, bravery implied something could go wrong. "I hope so."

Declan nodded at several of the others. "We're going to circle above. If we see anything suspicious, we'll return to our designated meeting place next to the castle," he told Birk.

It all sounded so well planned, and his calm delivery spoke of many accomplished missions. They discussed a few more details and then took flight. For some reason, Kyle was going to fly her to the castle entrance instead of Birk. She sensed that Birk's father or uncle suspected he might try to sabotage the escape.

"Ready to see if this invisibility shield works?" Kyle asked.

If it didn't, the plan would be called off. "I probably should have tried that before everyone arrived."

He shrugged. "I trust Fay."

She stuck her hand in her pocket, and her fingers touched the amulet. She removed it and placed it over her heart and mentally recited the words. *"Pure of soul, kind of heart, I shall be free to do my part."*

"Lily?"

When she blinked and looked down, she wasn't there. "I did it!"

Kyle smiled. "You did—but I have to say, hearing your voice when I can't see you is very strange."

Everyone had been worried she might not be able to be heard. Just in case that happened, she'd written out what she wanted each of the captives to do. Even now, she might pass the note as a way to communicate. She didn't need a guard overhearing an unfamiliar voice and investigating.

Kyle backed up, shifted, and then held out his claw. Unless she spoke, she had no idea if he'd know when she was securely in his grasp.

"I'm good," she said after she settled in for the ride.

Up he went. They flew over the castle and then landed in the field that bordered the forest in back. He set her down, and Lily crawled out of his grasp. Even though she wasn't touching him, he remained invisible. He must have cloaked himself.

"Wish me luck," she whispered.

Of course he couldn't answer, but it was just as well. Right now, she needed to focus on freeing the innocent white lighters. He said he would deposit her in back of the castle instead of the front, because there were fewer guards there.

What difference did that make since no one could see her? Lily jogged around to the side of the castle toward the entrance Finn had used to enter the basement. While she'd toured the place once when she was on a school trip, she hadn't remembered it being so expansive.

When Lily reached the designated door, she mentally ran through the first few turns: two lefts, three rights, and then one left. There was no need for panic. She had Finn's map in case she had the jitters. Oh, damn. If she were invisible, so would be the paper the instructions were written on. Hopefully, her memory didn't fail her.

Just as she reached to pull open the door, she stopped and looked around. The moment she touched it, it would disappear.

Having an entrance with no doorway could attract attention. Just then two tourists walked by, laughing and gawking, and pointed to something high on the castle. Once their backs were to her, Lily opened the door and slid inside.

Here goes.

The inside smelled of mold and what she could only guess was urine. It was quite disgusting.

Focus.

No guard was in sight, which helped Lily to relax. The first turn couldn't come soon enough. It was a left.

So far so good. After many more turns, she spotted the metal box on the wall that contained the keys, and she let out a breath. She hadn't taken any wrong turns—so far.

Moving quicker now that she'd made it without any incident, she continued. Voices sounded, and she plastered her back against the wall. The last thing she needed was for a guard to run into her— literally. If he did, she feared she might let out a moan and give away her position.

Two men rounded the corner and one man chuckled, totally oblivious to her presence. Thank you, Fay.

After making many more turns, she finally rounded the corner and spotted the jail cells. She did it! Her heart pounded as Lily glanced to each of the cells, trying to place the faces from the pictures. Not everyone would be saved. Some deserved to remain there.

One second she was congratulating herself on her achievement and the next she went flying, the force on her back driving her to her knees. With tremendous effort, she held in a shriek.

"What the fuck was that?" a deep voice said, sounding royally pissed.

Oh, shit. Lily crawled to the wall and slowly rose to her feet, praying they'd have no idea what the man had hit.

"What happened?" a second man asked.

"I don't know. It was like I hit a wall." The man who'd run into her scanned the cells.

"It was probably one of those fucking white lighters playing a trick on you," the other man said.

"Probably."

The guard who'd knocked her down swung his arms around, but thankfully she was out of his reach. The second guard nudged him. "Come on. The prince wants a report."

When both of them strode past the cells and disappeared from sight, Lily wasn't sure she could go on. Why in the hell did she think she was able to pull this off when the Guardians hadn't been able to?

She stuck her hands in her pockets and felt the three pieces of paper that had the instructions written on them. She studied those in the cells. All were thin, drawn, and quite filthy. Oh, my. Lily had to help them. Inhaling deeply to calm down, she had to hold in a cough. The mold and stench of unwashed bodies was assaulting her.

I can do this. I want to make Birk proud.

Lily walked up to the cell where the woman Kaleena had be-friended was being kept. Lily retrieved the instructions from her pocket, and then slid the invisible piece of paper through the bars. The moment she released it, the paper appeared.

Danita stilled and then smiled. It was as if she understood what was happening. She picked up the paper, read it, and then nodded. Thank goodness for white lighters. Magic was second nature for them.

Because Lily feared those who wouldn't be saved would make a fuss, the instructions made it clear that those she was helping were to say nothing—only nod if they understood what they needed to do.

Once all three received their instructions and agreed, Lily needed to open each cell door. Without that step, nothing would work. Starting with Danita's cell, Lily stuck the first key in the lock and twisted it. Of course, the cell door became invisible once the key touched it, making it harder to work. Nothing clicked. Too bad Lily couldn't tell if she'd used the wrong key or if the locks had been changed. On her fifth attempt, the lock finally turned, and relief rushed through her.

As soon as Lily removed the key, the door appeared. Lily looked right then left, to make sure no other guards were coming. "Stay here while I unlock the other doors," she whispered. Once more, Danita nodded.

After a few mishaps, Lily finally had all three doors opened. The man inside the cell farthest from Danita's was shaking. Lily wasn't sure if it was because he had no idea what was happening, or because he'd been abused and was weak. Lily grabbed his hand and led him out. Thankfully, he became invisible.

"Close the door," she whispered.

"Who are you?" he asked.

"It doesn't matter. Now be quiet, and whatever you do, don't let go."

He squeezed her hand as if to let her know he understood. She opened the second door. This time, the frail woman was smart enough to grab hold of the man's hand. She moaned a little and then followed unseen.

Oh, shit. "Pick up the paper so there is no evidence," Lily whispered.

Back they went to the first man's cell.

"Hey," yelled one of the prisoners who she wasn't supposed to help.

Shit. He couldn't see her or anyone else, but he could hear her. She then remembered that the door had squeaked when she'd pulled it open. Lily could only hope the man holding her hand didn't respond.

"I heard his cell open. Who are you?" the prisoner called out again.

"Shh." Lily hadn't meant to give away her position, but she couldn't help it.

"I know you're there. You've got to help me. I'm here against my will. Please. Open my cell."

Damn. He wasn't one of the ones who deserved his freedom. As much as Lily was tempted to help, she had to free Danita and then get the hell out of there before the guards came.

The problem was that Danita had a set of cuffs on her wrists like the ones they had used on Kaleena when she had been held captive.

She stepped from the cell, but then grunted. Damn. As much as Lily wanted to move fast, she couldn't chance someone letting go.

Footsteps sounded. "Hey, what's all the yelling about," one of the guards said to the man in the cell.

"I think someone escaped," he said.

Lily's muscles froze. She moved her train of people against the wall, but from the resistance, one of the prisoners wasn't able to move as quickly as she would have liked. It was probably Danita. Thankfully, none of them said anything.

The guard ran down the length of the cells. "Hey," the guard shouted. "Three of the prisoners have escaped. What the fuck?"

She and her crew made it around the corner and couldn't see what the second guard was doing—but she could hear the panic in their voices. Very slowly, she moved sideways edging her way farther from the corner. If they could make it to the first turn, they might be safe.

"Spread out," a second guard shouted. "They couldn't have gone far."

Oh, how had Lily believed she could pull this off—even with an invisibility amulet?

One of the women at the end of the line moaned, and Lily stilled.

"I'll look down this corridor," the first guard said.

"I'll check out the other one," the other guard called out. It was where they were.

With their backs against the wall, Lily thought it best not to move in the hopes he'd travel down the middle of the hallway. Given these were white lighters, he probably figured they could cloak themselves. It might be why he was waving his arms, hoping to run into one.

Please don't let him find us.

What seemed like an eternity, the guard returned and swept past them. Lily prayed that Birk and the men weren't out there freaking, wondering what was taking so long.

Once the guard was out of sight, Lily squeezed the man's hand. He in turn must have passed on the signal that it was time to move. As much as Lily wanted to walk quickly, she had to take care not to stress the escapees.

They were probably halfway to the exit, when a female voice rang out. Lily stopped and looked behind her. Crap. Danita was on the ground, head down, and very visible.

"Grab her hand," Lily demanded of the woman who had been holding it.

"Sorry," Danita whispered. "I tripped."

A moment later, Danita was invisible once more. Better understanding what weakness could do to a person, Lily waited until the man squeezed Lily's hand before she continued. This time, she walked even slower.

What seemed like a million hours later, they finally reached the exterior door where Birk and several of his relatives would be waiting for them. She turned around. "Don't let go until I tell you."

They grumbled their response. She touched the door to open it, and it immediately disappeared. Lily led her entourage outside. All three whimpered, probably because of the fresh air and warmth of the sun on their faces.

The Guardians had to be somewhere and had hopefully seen the door temporarily disappear. Lily looked up, hoping to see some colorful dragons, but she didn't spot anyone. Damn.

One moment she was shielding her eyes against the sun's glare, and the next she was up in the air. Oh, no. The three prisoners were now visible. Lily struggled. How had this dragon known where she was? Whoever *he* was. Was it Birk, her brother, or some Royal Guard?

When she lost sight of the escaped prisoners, she clasped the dragon's talons harder. If this wasn't Birk, she had to let him know she'd been taken. Lily rubbed the ring, and the dragon slowed and headed to the ground.

He set her down on shaky legs and then shifted. When she saw it was Birk, she ran to him.

"Oh, baby. I'm so sorry to have scared you like that." He hugged her and kissed her hair.

"I thought it might be you, but I couldn't be sure," she said, her chin trembling.

"You are amazing."

She didn't feel so amazing right now. The prisoners had been the brave ones, trusting her like they had. Wanting to be seen again, she pressed the amulet to her heart and recited the words. When she became visible, Birk smiled. He kissed her lips lightly. "You taste good."

Silly man. "How did you know where I was just now? I was invisible."

"Because I was close by, the tracking device allowed me to hone in on you. What you didn't see was how slowly I approached. I didn't want to barrel into you."

"Thank you." All of this was too much to grasp. "I can't believe we did it." Her chin trembled and a few salty tears trickled down her cheek.

"All that matters is that you are safe."

"What about the escapees?" she asked. "Where are they?"

"They will be taken someplace safe."

"To the mine?"

Birk smiled and dragged a knuckle down her cheek. "No, we can't chance them seeing our facility, but rest assured they will be well taken care of."

"Thank you."

"Ready to head back to SinCas?"

Lily tried not to show her disappointment. She wanted to clean up and snuggle with Birk. "Why do we need to go there?"

"We always debrief after a mission."

A mission. She liked the sound of that. She'd run a mission. "Then fly away, dragon-boy."

Chapter Seventeen

BIRK COULD TELL Lily wanted to go home and relax, but her knowledge of what occurred inside the castle could help others in the future. Had his dad not asked him to take her to SinCas to fill everyone in, Birk would have given in to her wishes.

Once there, Birk escorted Lily down the stairwell and into the conference room. As soon as they stepped inside, party streamers sounded and horns tooted.

"Whoa. What's going on?" To his surprise, almost everyone in the family was there—except for those taking care of the former prisoners.

His dad came up to Lily and hugged her. "Congratulations. You did a great thing today, young lady."

Lily tightened her grip on Birk's hand, acting as if she wasn't comfortable with the praise. "I couldn't have done it without Fay and the Four Sisters, as well as the rest of you."

Laird smiled. "It was mostly you. Come on and take a seat. We can debrief in a moment."

Lily looked up at Birk. "I can't believe they did this. No one has ever thrown a party for me before."

The excitement in her eyes and voice made up for all the agony she'd put him through since she started on this mission. "Me neither. Let's get something to drink," he said.

"Just water for me. Right now, my adrenaline is surging through me so fast, if I had coffee or an alcoholic drink, I'd be pinging off the walls."

"Water it is. Sit down and I'll bring it to you."

While he fixed the drinks, his mom carried over a cake and handed Lily a knife. "You want to do the honors?"

"Sure, but what would you have done if the escape had failed? Would you have hidden the cake?"

Birk set the drinks in front of her.

His mom smiled. "Failure wasn't an option. We're Guardians, remember?" She winked.

For the next hour, Lily answered their questions, most of which came from Kaleena. "You said Danita was weak?"

"Yes, she was wearing metal cuffs, like the ones you said you'd worn."

"Asshole Royals." She shook her head. "And here I thought with Rathan dead, the evil would stop. I hope Declan takes her to the Four Sisters so they can remove those poisonous restraints."

"I'll text Declan now." Birk pulled out his phone and sent a short message. "Done."

After Lily told everyone as much as she remembered, Birk pushed back his chair. Lily's skin looked a bit pale, and her shoulders were slumped. "I think Lily would like to rest."

"Of course," his dad said. "Once I have the full update from Declan about the condition of the prisoners, I'll let you know."

After they congratulated Lily once more on a job well done, Birk escorted her out. "Food first or shower?"

She chuckled. "For someone with a good sense of smell, I'm surprised you have to ask. How about I shower and we order in some burgers?"

"It's a deal."

The trip back to his place took mere seconds. Lily seemed tired but happy when he set her down. Once in his condo, she headed straight for the bathroom.

"How do you want your hamburger cooked?" he called after her.

"Medium rare. And order some fries, please. I'm in the mood to live dangerously."

Birk chuckled. The person he'd first met had been shy and tentative. After this successful mission, Lily was more exuberant than ever.

The water turned on in the shower, and as much as he wanted to join her, he figured she needed the time to decompress and think about what really happened. Having someone run into her had scared not only her, but Birk as well. Until they finally mated, Birk was not going to let her out of his sight.

Once he called for their dinner delivery, Birk waited for Lily to finish cleaning up. A few moments after the water shut off, the doorbell rang. He paid for the meal, and then placed the food on the table. A second later, Lily walked out, dressed in cute pink pajamas and drying her hair with a towel.

His animal went wild. Birk's skin nearly became covered in ruby red pulsing scales.

"Something smells amazing," she said, seemingly unaware of how much he wanted her.

Birk smiled and motioned to the table. "Sit and let's eat. I'm starving."

Lily pulled out a chair and sat across from him. "How can you be so hungry? You ate three pieces of cake at the party."

He laughed. "Dragons are always hungry." *And this dragon is particularly hungry for you.*

"Thank you," she said.

"For what?" She couldn't have read his mind.

"For being so supportive. I know you must have been crazy with worry the whole time I was inside the castle."

"Only a little." Birk had hidden in the woods, far enough so as not to be seen by any guard, but close enough should he sense she was in danger.

He curled his fingers around his glass, not wanting her to see that he'd bitten his nails down to the quick during the hour long escape. Birk wasn't used to standing by while someone he loved put herself in danger. He kept telling himself that Lily needed to do this. Her selfless act spoke volumes for who she was as a person. While he didn't picture her doing battle once they mated—despite the fact she would possess great power like her brother—she would be a valuable asset to the Guardians.

"You're lying," she said with a twinkle in her eyes.

"Am I? How do you know?"

"Your eyes turn dark when you aren't telling the truth."

Really? No one had ever told him that before. Lily laughed, stuffed a bite of hamburger into her mouth, and chewed. Once she finished, she leaned back. "You would be a lot happier in life if you didn't worry so much. How many times were you tempted to rush into the castle and save me—even though I wasn't in trouble?"

"About once every minute."

She chuckled. "See? I know you well."

Lily had his number all right. Seeing her so calm after what she'd accomplished said a lot about her. He dug into the meal and relaxed for the first time in a while.

"If you want to shower, I can clean up here," Lily said.

He probably did need to wash. "I'd appreciate that."

Birk loved how comfortable she seemed around him now. It was almost as if they had mated. As she dumped the paper bag in the trash and placed the glasses in the sink, he stepped into his room and discarded his clothes. Once the water warmed, he ducked under the hot stream and washed away all the worry that had built up in his system. Just as he'd finished rinsing, his bedroom door opened.

"Lily?"

Of course it was her. It wasn't a dragon shifter. With the water running, he couldn't be sure what she was doing until the bathroom door opened and a naked Lily stepped in. Instantly, his teeth sharpened and his scales glowed.

Mate, mate, his dragon chanted.

He wanted Lily worse than anything, but she wasn't ready for mating. Today was the first time she'd experienced what life with him would be like—full of danger and adventure. While she did exceptionally well, she needed time to come to grips with everything, and what could have happened if something had gone wrong.

"I was wondering if you needed help," she said as she moved closer to the shower door.

"I absolutely do. Seeing your luscious body has made me totally forget how to use this bar of soap." It didn't matter that he'd already washed.

She grinned, just as he'd hoped she would. Lily entered the stall and held out her hand. "Then let me wash you."

Heaven help me. All during the mission, Birk tried to distract himself by thinking of the moment when he could make love to this amazing woman again. Now that it was about to come true once more, he wanted to take his time and savor every inch of her body.

She slipped the soap from his fingers. "Turn around," she said.

Birk obeyed and palmed the wall in front of him. She moved him away from the spray. As soon as her gentle fingers massaged his shoulders, and then his back, and finally his butt, he had to concentrate on not dragging her out of the shower and impaling her.

"Other side," she commanded.

He wasn't sure he could take much more of her touching, but he obeyed. When she soaped up his cock and stroked it, he groaned. "Lily."

As if he hadn't spoken, she continued to wash his very hard dick, making sure to clean his balls too. She was a temptress all right, one he couldn't resist.

When she placed the soap on the shelf and rubbed her hands higher on his chest, his ability to keep from touching her cracked. Without any thought to getting her soapy, Birk drew her close and kissed her hard. His hands found her sweet ass, and when he rubbed her butt, his scales glowed and his body heated. As much as he wanted to drive his cock into her, he had to rinse off first.

He'd do that in just a few more seconds. Their tongues entwined, and he savored her sweet taste that had a hint of meat and tomato.

After they thoroughly devoured each other, he stepped back and did a final rinse. "I think we need to find a new location for what I have in mind."

She cocked a brow. "What's that?"

"It's a surprise." Birk turned off the water and then held open the shower door for her. Once she stepped on the blue nubby bath mat, he grabbed a towel. She then slid the white one from the rack, but he stopped her. Tossing the towel she'd grabbed over his shoulder he dragged the one he'd snatched down her chest. "Let me dry you off."

"What are you trying to do? Convince me to have sex with you?"

Birk cracked up. "If I need to convince you then I've been doing something very wrong."

Lily moved closer and ran a nail down his wet chest. "Seems to me that you haven't done much of anything yet."

That did it. He dropped the towel in his hand, lifted her up in a fireman's hold, and then stomped into his bedroom. If she hadn't been laughing and pounding on his back, he would have put her down instantly.

Once in the bedroom, Birk slipped her off his shoulders. "I think the mission of freeing the prisoners was a bad idea."

Lily looked up at him, all innocent like. "How can you say that?"

"Because you never gave me this much sass before. For your punishment, I want you to stand perfectly still while I enjoy looking at you."

"That won't be a problem, but are you sure you don't want me to do more?" She dropped her gaze to his hard cock.

"You're asking for it."

"You're pretty smart for such a big guy."

Using the towel from over his shoulder, he dragged a portion over her breasts again and then dried her stomach.

"You're taking too long," she said, attempting to grab the towel.

Birk stopped her. "Oh no you don't. You promised to stand still."

"You're stalling."

"What's wrong? Do you have no will power?"

Lily furrowed her brows and pursed her lips. She then crossed her arms over her chest. "I know what you're trying to do. Go ahead, dragon-boy. See if you can turn me on."

"Dragon-boy? In case you haven't noticed, I am all man." Birk couldn't help but grab his stiff cock and wave it at her.

She laughed. "You are so easy to tease."

He wouldn't take her bait any longer. Birk knelt and dried off her right leg and then her left, avoiding the area between her legs, believing she was dying to have him touch her there. "Turn around."

She did, and he couldn't help but notice how she'd stiffened. Regardless of the number of times he'd told her that the scars on her back meant nothing to him, he'd failed to convince her. Birk stood and patted her back dry. Dropping the terrycloth towel on the floor, he leaned over and kissed her neck and then inhaled deeply. "I love how you smell," he said, unable to keep the awe and need from his voice.

Lily must have decided not to play coy anymore for she slipped her hands behind her and grabbed his ass. His dick pressed hard against her, sending off another strong wave of need through him. With each kiss and nibble, her fingers tightened on his skin.

"You're right, Birk."

He continued working his way from her ear down to her shoulder. "About what?"

"That I can't stand still when you touch me. My body is already on fire."

Birk spun her around. "Is that so?"

"I'll show you."

She drew his head down and kissed him like there was no tomorrow. Their tongues crashed into each other, and she pressed her tits hard against his body. He threaded his fingers through her slightly wet hair and tugged hard. "Need you," he whispered after leaning back.

"I need you too."

Backing her up until she was pressed against the bedroom door,

Birk dropped to his knees and spread her legs wide.

"First, I feast," he said.

She groaned. "Don't take too long. My pussy is already throbbing."

"I'll do my best." He had no intention of letting her off the hook this easily. From the moment he had laid eyes on her, he had been the one to suffer from wanting her. It was about time she yearned for him as much.

Birk leaned over and swiped his tongue across her opening to give her a taste of what was to come, but he was the one who paid the price. His dick turned even harder and his scales glowed in more places than he thought possible.

Drawing on his Guardian strength and control, he slipped two fingers into her wetness and had to clamp his mouth together to keep his teeth from elongating any farther.

Lily moaned and then swayed, but it was when she grabbed his hair and tugged that he nearly lost it.

When Birk's tongue found her clit and gently sucked on it, she arched her back and let out a sexy little cry. He only stopped because her knees buckled.

Birk shot to his feet and held her up by the waist. "Are you okay?" he asked.

She finally opened her eyes. "I think so. When my climax rushed in, I was overwhelmed with incredible heat."

He couldn't help but smile. "I have just the remedy," he said.

She looked up at him and clasped his shoulders. "What's that?"

"Wrap your legs around my waist, and I'll show you."

He lifted her up and held her at waist height until she did as he asked. With her back pressed against the door and her tits flattened on his chest, Birk couldn't hold out any longer. He threaded his cock into her opening, and to his delight, her slick entry allowed easy access.

Her eyes widened, acting as if his size was larger than she expected. Without a word, Lily pressed the soles of her feet against his thighs, rose up, and then eased her way down. "That feels so fucking good," she murmured.

Birk almost chuckled at her crass comment, hoping there would be more dirty talk in the future. "We've only just begun."

She slid her hands to his face and kissed him again. Birk's hands dropped to her waist, and he held her up while he plowed into her. He went fast for a few strokes and then agonizingly slow. With each change in speed, Lily moaned, and her pussy turned slicker.

As she slid her tongue around his, Birk held her tighter, trying to keep his rapid heartbeat in check. This was testing his resolve to the max.

When she broke the kiss and dropped her lips to his neck, visions of him sinking his teeth into her surfaced. But he had to wait. It wasn't fair to her if he didn't.

Lily once more took control of the rhythm, and he let her have her way. After all, she'd been through a lot today. Too bad it was driving his dragon to the breaking point.

Wanting better access to her body, he spun around, and in three long steps, reached the bed. He dropped her on the tangled sheets with him still buried deep inside her.

She wrapped her arms around his neck. "Did I ever tell you that I think I love you?"

Birk's mouth turned dry, and his pulse soared. He never thought he'd ever hear those words from her mouth. "No."

See? You can mate with her now, his dragon said. *Lily wants you to.*

Not yet. She only thinks she loves me. I want her to be sure.

Birk pressed his head against her neck and thrust deep into her. Once fully inside, he held perfectly still to quell his raging need.

Lily planted her feet on the mattress and lifted up. "Yes, Birk, yes!"

He lost it. With his climax brimming, he plunged into her again and again. From the way she'd clamped down hard on his cock, and the fact her eyes had rolled back into her head, she'd climaxed, and

Birk was only a few seconds behind.

Once he'd pumped his hot seed into her, Lily's body sagged, and they lay in each other's arms for a long while. Without a word, he slipped out and retrieved a washcloth to clean her up. He loved having Lily with him, next to him, around him—forever.

Chapter Eighteen

LILY AWOKE TO find herself snuggled against Birk's body, and she smiled. He was snoring soundly, and while she didn't have the heart to wake him, she did lightly run her fingers over his shoulder, marveling at how lucky she was to end up with such an amazing man.

Not wanting to disturb him, she eased out of the bed, washed up, and then returned to her bedroom to dress. He'd fixed her breakfast the last few times, so it was her turn. Okay, he had ordered the food from a local restaurant, but that was beside the point. She owned a phone and could call too.

At some point, she'd suggest they take that shopping trip to the grocery store he'd promised her. She liked to cook and wanted to make some tantalizing meals for Birk. The number of his favorite breakfast place was on a magnet stuck to the side of the fridge, so she called in an order. He told her he used the Egg Hatchery often and had checked out the delivery boys. They'd been given permission to enter the secure building.

Hopefully, Birk would be up before they arrived. Opening the door to a stranger might not be wise.

Lily had just set the table when sounds of Birk stirring reached her. She was tempted to walk into his room and seduce him again, but with her luck, the food would come sooner rather than later.

Birk's cell phone rang and a minute later he pushed open his bedroom door, cell phone still pressed against his ear.

"We'll be there as soon as we can, Dad. Oh, okay. An hour then."

Birk disconnected, and from the way his jaw had tightened, the news wasn't good. "What is it?" she asked.

He spun to face her. "Toma contacted us."

She reached behind her to grab the dining room chair, fearing she might fall. With everything that had happened, she'd almost forgotten about the threat on her life. "What did he say?"

"The man who wants you contacted him."

Her stomach nearly revolted. "But he can't have me."

Birk closed the space between them and gathered her into his strong arms. "No, he can't. I won't let that happen."

A knock sounded on the door and she jumped. Birk inhaled. "Did you order breakfast? I smell eggs."

Wow. His sense of smell was amazing. "Yes."

The deliveryman knocked again. "I'll get it," he said.

She let him pay since he would insist anyway. Birk placed the food on the table while she fixed the coffee. "What else did your dad say?" Lily tried to sound as casual as possible, but she really didn't think she succeeded.

"I don't know all of the details, but apparently, the man who has Toma's daughters called him to let him know his time was up."

Something wasn't right. "Toma is in jail. How can he have a phone?"

"He doesn't, but my cousin Anderson Caspian, who works for the Avonbelle Province Police, made arrangements for Toma to receive calls in case the man who has Toma's daughters called him."

"What did this guy say exactly?"

"Why don't you have some breakfast first, and then we'll head on over to SinCas. My dad, Uncle Jamison, and Declan have come up with a plan. They'll fill you in."

Lily wondered if this was what Birk's life was always like. "Don't you ever have a break? I mean, first you have to protect me from that guy after Nessa and now this."

He smiled as he reached across the table and rubbed a thumb across the back of her hand. "It's not always this busy. I do have a job that requires me to keep the mines free of any disturbances, but trouble seems to come in waves lately. Eat up."

Even though her appetite had basically disappeared, Lily didn't know the next time food would be available. She told herself she had total faith in the Guardians, but somehow, her stomach wasn't buying it.

Once they had more or less finished their meal and cleaned up, Birk flew her over to the SinCas building. This trip was becoming all too familiar, and the dread that had once occupied her body returned. The Guardians would protect her, but being the target scared the crap out of her.

This time when Lily entered the conference room, she was met with solemn faces instead of a party atmosphere. Birk had only mentioned three people would be there, but a lot more had come, all looking at her, as if they expected her to fall apart. She didn't recognize one man and looked up at Birk.

"This is my oldest brother, Griffin."

She tried to smile. "Nice to meet you."

"You too."

Birk placed a hand on her back and led her over to the table where pitchers of water sat in the middle.

"Good, everyone is here," Jamison Sinclair said. "I'll bring you up to speed, Lily. We've been aware for quite some time that a loan shark, by the name of Richard Dorlack, is into everything from human trafficking to money laundering."

"If you've identified him as someone who engages in illegal activities, why can't you or the police take him down?" As soon as the question left her lips, Lily realized it was a stupid question. "You need to catch him in the act, right? That's where I come in." Well, damn.

He tossed her a quick smile. "We've been trying to catch him, but the man is rather illusive."

"He's a dragon shifter, isn't he?" Lily asked. Birk hadn't been sure.

"We've recently learned that he is, but that alone doesn't make him bad, honey."

Lily wanted to sink into her seat. "I didn't mean it that way."

Birk cupped her hand. "We know."

Jamison nodded. "Dorlack is unaware that Toma is in jail, and we want to keep it that way. We needed Dorlack to reach out to him. It's why Toma has been kept in solitary."

Good. "So now what?" She looked around the room, but she couldn't read anyone's expression.

"That's what we're here for. Declan and I have been discussing tactics. Dorlack demanded that Toma deliver you to a warehouse in Glen Meadow at five this evening or Toma's two daughters will be sold."

Her stomach soured, and bile burned her throat. "Those poor girls. They must be out of their mind with grief and fear. What are you going to do?" she asked, knowing full well Birk wouldn't let her be given to this man.

Tory piped up. "I'm going in your place. We look enough alike to fool most people."

"No way. It will be too dangerous," Lily blurted.

Tory cocked an eye. "At least I'm a dragon with excellent fighting skills. You aren't. But even if I pretend to be you, there will be issues. For one, I'm taller. I can only slump over so far without making it look obvious."

"Who's to say this Dorlack person knows how tall I am?" Lily said.

Tory smiled. "Let's hope he doesn't, unless the photo of you was taken when you were standing next to Toma."

"I wasn't even aware anyone was at Toma's place other than the two of us." She glanced over at Birk. "I didn't see Birk until he charged out of the woods."

His dad seemed to be fighting a smile.

"Height aside, we both have the same color hair, and I'll wear mine like you do. I figure with a hat and a pair of sunglasses, I should be good," Tory said, sounding very professional.

"What about your dragon signature?" Birk asked. "The moment you meet Dorlack, he'll know there's been a bait and switch."

Tory waved a finger at him. "I plan to ask Magnolia if she can give me the same signature cloaking stone she gave Nessa."

Lily couldn't help but wonder how successful the Guardians would be without these pottery ladies. Were they somehow connected to the Guardians? Relatives perhaps?

Griffin pushed back his chair. "I'll head on over there now and ask them for the stone. Nessa and Tory need to stay here since they are part of the plan."

Lily had yet to hear the details of this crazy scheme.

"Good luck," Jamison said. "Without it, we may have to change our tactic."

Griffin nodded and left.

"Let me get this straight," Lily said. "Tory pretends to be me. What happens when she and Toma arrive at the designated place? Once Dorlack realizes there's been a switch, he'll kill her."

"We won't let it get that far," Jamison said. "We have to assume that Dorlack has men watching our every move. They might even know that you're in here with us now."

A cold shiver raced down her spine. "What are you saying?"

Declan leaned forward. "It's why we would like you to go with Toma until you are close to Glen Meadow."

Her breath whooshed out. "I don't trust him. What's to stop him from killing me? Or incapacitating me?"

"He needs you," Declan said. "If he doesn't turn you over, his daughters will die."

"But you said Tory will take my place." Lily thought she had understood, but apparently she hadn't.

"Yes, she will, but we don't want to tip off Toma too soon. You and she will change places at a gas station close to Glen Meadow. Toma will be told to stop there."

"What if he doesn't?"

Birk clasped her hand. "I'll stop the truck and make him turn around if he doesn't. Besides, he'll want to gas up. Once he has his daughters, he'll want to make it back to town without stopping."

"Don't worry," Jamison said. "Neither you nor Tory will ever be alone. Our men will fly overhead. Sometimes they will be in their cloaked form, and at other times they won't."

"What's to stop Dorlack from killing Tory the second he realizes she's not me?" She'd asked that before, but the answer didn't satisfy her.

Declan shook his head. "We'll instruct Toma to keep Tory in the truck until he is positive his daughters are alive. That may or may not be what happens, but we'll be ready for any contingency."

Tory tapped the table. "If I do have to get out of the truck, and if I am recognized, I'll shift into my dragon form. Dorlack is a dragon, and even if he has several of his men with him, I can fend them off for a few seconds until everyone else arrives."

"It's dangerous."

Tory nodded. "It is, but it's what we have to do."

They spent the next hour going over the strategy. If they expected Toma to arrive in Glen Meadow by five, they had to leave soon. Right before the departure time, Griffin returned and handed the stone to Tory.

"How did Magnolia seem?" Tory asked.

"She was hesitant at first, but when I explained what had happened, she gave it to me. Like before, it comes with the twenty-four hour expiration."

"I'll stop in and thank her when I get back," Tory said.

That was one hurdle jumped. Lily looked down at her pink shirt and Tory's blue one. "We aren't dressed the same."

Kaleena, who'd left a while ago, returned with two bags, almost as if she was waiting for someone to mention it. "Sorry I took so long." She handed Tory and Lily each a bag. "I decided to go with jeans, a white T-shirt, sandals, and a cute pink hat. I hope I guessed your size, Lily. Why don't you two go into the bathroom and change? I tossed in some makeup, hairbrushes, and clips. Try to look as alike as possible."

This was like a bad dream. If things went according to plan, Lily would be safely hidden in some gas station bathroom while Tory would be out there fighting dragons—all to save some scumbag's daughters. True, his daughters were innocent, but it was a lot to ask of Tory—Guardian or not.

With their bags in hand, they entered the SinCas building bathroom, and Tory locked the door for privacy. They undressed and changed into their matching clothes. They both decided to keep things simple by pulling their hair into a ponytail. They then put on the same color lipstick, the same shade of blush, the pink hat, and sunglasses. When they stood next to each other, they both smiled.

"I have to admit that at first glance, we could be twins," Lily said.

Tory bent her knees so they were the same height and the similarity increased. "Let's hope they don't remember how tall you are. If someone is watching, when you get in the car with Toma, pull down your cap and bend over."

"That will make me even shorter," Lily said.

"True, but it disguises your real height."

Lily practiced slumping and pulling the hat over her eyes. She then spun toward Tory. "I can't tell you how much I appreciate this. I don't know what I would have done if Toma tried to turn me over to that horrible man."

Tory smiled. "First off, Birk wouldn't let that happen."

Lily nodded. "I know."

"Don't look so glum. Nothing will go wrong. The men will watch Toma's every move. He will be told that if he doesn't stop at the prescribed gas station, we won't prevent his daughters from being sold. That's not true, but he won't know that."

It still didn't set well with her. "Thank you again."

"Come on. We don't have much time."

"Am I supposed to sit in the gas station bathroom until the

fighting is over?" she asked.

"I would wait at least ten minutes before coming out in case someone becomes suspicious. Nessa and Logan will be there, ready to drive you back to Edendale. Once we arrive at the warehouse, all hell will break loose. I imagine they won't be worrying about where you are."

"Where will Birk be?" She hadn't meant for her voice to waver, but Lily was used to having him around.

Tory looked off to the side. "He was torn. He wanted to stay with you, but he trusts Nessa and Logan." Tory looked to the side.

"What is it?"

"If you want my opinion, Birk has this driving need to eliminate Dorlack. The fact the man wants you is eating away at my cousin. He won't rest until the man is dead."

Or until Birk is dead. "I get it."

When they entered the conference room, several jaws dropped. Tory raised her arms. "Well? Other than me towering over her, what do you think?"

Birk pushed back his chair. "It's amazing. It will take a hard look to tell the difference. If you are in a car with tinted windows, you should be good."

Jamison and Laird stood. "Time to go, guys," Jamison announced.

Birk rushed up to Lily. "How are you holding up?"

She loved the concern in his voice. "I'm fine. While I don't like driving a few hours in a car with Toma, once he drops me off, I'll be good."

Birk hugged her, and all of her worry washed away. "I'll make sure nothing happens to you."

"I know. How far is this warehouse from the gas station?"

"It's about a seven-minute drive," Birk said. "We wanted you close in case Dorlack tried anything at the last minute."

"Tory told me to wait ten minutes before leaving the bathroom," she said.

"That's smart."

They took the elevator down to the first floor, while the rest headed up to the roof.

"Are you sure you're okay with this?" Birk asked.

She looked up at him. "I can't say no. I don't want to be responsible for those two women being sold, but I'm not really the one at risk. Tory is."

He smiled down at her. "Tory will be fine."

Birk stopped at the front door. "Where are we going?" she asked.

"See that large black truck?"

Shit. The name Toma Construction was plastered on the side. "He's really free." It was a statement, not a question.

"For now. We are responsible for returning him. We are assuming that Dorlack's men are watching even now. Cross the street as if you are heading to the café. Toma will jump out of the truck and place an unloaded gun to your back. He'll force you into the passenger's seat. Struggle some, but not overly so. We don't want to draw the attention of any do-gooders."

No one had explained this to her before. "What if he ties me up? Or knocks me out?" Her pulse shot up thinking about the restriction.

"He doesn't want you harmed in any way. Remember, you are his ticket to getting his daughters back."

"Does he know about the switch at the gas station?"

"No. I'm hoping he won't notice because he'll be too nervous and anxious to see his daughters again."

She shook her head. "You're giving this scum a lot of credit. I'm not so sure he cares all that much for them. He probably just wants the chance to join forces with Dorlack."

Birk stroked her face. "Stop worrying. We have this covered." Birk leaned over and kissed her. "Remember that I love you."

He loved her? "Really? You're not just saying that to calm me down?"

He tapped her nose and smiled. "No. I didn't tell you before because I didn't think you were ready to hear it."

"I'm always ready to hear it," she said.

"I'll remember that. And speaking of remembering, all you have to do is rub that ring I gave you, and I'll be there in a flash. Camden will be tracking your every move."

Without thinking, she touched it. "I'll remember."

He swatted her butt. "Now go. And I'll see you soon."

Chapter Nineteen

B IRK WATCHED LILY cross the street. To the casual observer she acted fairly relaxed, but to him, she was scared. He couldn't point to one action, but her gate wasn't as fluid as usual, and her hands were stuffed in her pockets, probably hiding clenched fists.

Her thumb must have touched her ring, because an ache clamped down on his heart. Hard.

Oh, Lily, Lily. I wish I were with you right now.

He would be following her shortly—just as soon as Toma *escorted* her to his truck at gunpoint. Birk couldn't imagine what would have gone through her mind if that ass had really been kidnapping her.

If this rescue mission had involved anyone other than his mate, Birk wouldn't have worried nearly as much. It didn't matter that Lily had proven her worth under pressure when she saved those incarcerated at the prison. As much as Birk wanted to abort this mission, he wouldn't. He had to have faith that things would go according to plan.

Just as he'd instructed, Lily approached the café and then bent over as if to read the menu in the storefront window. Toma's truck door opened, and he glanced both ways before approaching her. As if he was meeting an old friend, Toma moved next to her—too close for Birk's comfort—and wrapped an arm around her shoulders. Lily stiffened but didn't call out.

Birk's fingers almost extended into talons. He wanted to punch the wall so badly—or more accurately, he wanted to punch Toma's face.

Lily twisted toward Toma and hate poured out of her eyes. Toma leaned in closer and said something to her. Acting as if Dorlack's men were near, she nodded. Good girl. Toma lowered his arm to around her waist and escorted her to his truck. He opened the passenger side door and shoved Lily inside.

Birk grabbed the handle to the front door. It was one thing to make it appear as if Toma was really kidnapping Lily, and it was another to hurt her. Once inside the vehicle, Birk expected her to rub her ring, but she must have realized that if Birk sensed her fear, he'd run out to the street, tear open the door, and drag her to safety.

And she'd be right.

Toma's truck took off, and Birk rushed to the elevator to head to the top floor. Even though he could fly faster than Toma's truck could drive, and most of the Guardians had a visual on it already, he needed to be doing something.

The elevator finally arrived and two people stepped out. Once the cage emptied, he rushed in and pressed the button for the top floor. He had suggested they turn one of the two elevators into an express that only went to the top floor, but so far that hadn't happened yet. The cab stopped on the third floor, and he forced himself to be polite to the lab tech who entered and was also going up.

Once they reached the fourth floor, Birk jumped out, dashed down the hallway, and then ran up the stairs to the rooftop. He shifted quickly, and as he flapped his wings to take off, he was met head-on by some incredible force. What the hell?

Stunned, he staggered backward, unable to sense another dragon. What was out there? A dark lighter? Or a well-cloaked dragon with a special ability to be undetected? Kyle's former assistant had the ability to become invisible, but that was the only person he'd heard of with that capability—and he was now dead.

Something sharp poked him in the chest, and his instinct kicked in. Birk lashed out, clawing and shooting fire at the unseen creature. It screamed, and its shield flickered, but it wasn't enough for Birk to determine what he looked like. Whatever or whoever it was had probably been sent by Dorlack. That meant this being had to die.

Going on the assumption this wasn't a dragon but rather some kind of demon, Birk shot upward and hovered above the rooftop. Not being able to see or sense his attacker made his choices more difficult. All he could do was dive and hope to incapacitate him. With his head down, Birk shot back to the rooftop and sent out an ear-shattering screech. As he landed, he whipped his tail back and forth, hoping to meet with some resistance—only he didn't.

Birk changed into human form, allowing him to do a more thorough search. If someone attacked him again, he could shift in a flash.

Trying to sense some presence, Birk stilled. All he could hear was the traffic four floors below. As much as he didn't want to waste precious time hunting this creature down, Birk needed to understand what kind of trickery he was up against. Behind the air conditioner on the south side of the building, he found a grappling hook attached to a rope. He looked over the edge but spotted no one. Had the rope been pulled taut, he would have unhooked it and let it drop.

Damn. If not a dragon then what? The slight disintegration of his cloaked shield didn't give Birk enough of an indication. He wanted to warn the others to be aware of strange happenings, but he couldn't contact anyone while in flight. Thankfully, he hadn't experienced any pain from Lily, which implied she was okay.

Birk was unwilling to spend any more time on this force of evil. If the purpose of the invisible attack was to delay him, it had failed. If somebody or something ambushed him on the way though, he'd be ready.

Birk shifted once more and took off. The trip from Edendale to Glen Meadow would take Toma four hours to drive, giving Birk time to catch up. There was the only road that connected the two places, so it didn't take Birk long to spot the truck.

Birk and the team suspected that Dorlack's goons would be in the air hovering overhead to make sure Toma had safe passage.

They'd have no reason to interfere since they wanted what was in his car. What they probably wouldn't tolerate was for anyone else to be nearby. That meant the Guardians couldn't show their faces—or rather their dragon selves.

When Birk sensed a Guardian—who had a different signature than other shifters—he pulled back. Because he didn't trust himself not to let his emotions get the best of him, he headed to the gas station where Toma was to stop.

With a few hours to go before they arrived, Birk decided to do a cloaked fly-by of Glen Meadow. Understanding the terrain would make fighting and hiding easier. Dorlack had given Toma a specific location for the transfer, so that was where Birk headed.

No surprise, the warehouse was in a rather isolated location. Birk sensed a few dragons and spotted several more visible ones doing surveillance. In case that invisible creature was there, Birk kept his distance. Waiting was not his strong point, especially where Lily was involved.

ONCE TOMA JUMPED into the driver's seat, he leaned over and slapped a pair of cuffs on Lily's left wrist and attached the other end to the grip handle above the door, so that she had no ability to face him.

"Why are you doing that?" she demanded.

"I need to make it look good."

Now she was forced to sit looking out the window or chance dislocating her shoulder. Asshole. "I'm here voluntarily, you know."

Toma glanced over at her. "That's what worries me. Something's up. Birk Caspian isn't going to let me turn you over to Dorlack."

She'd been coached what to say. "You will get your girls and then turn me over. That's when Birk and his men will swoop in and save the day." She was pleased her voice didn't catch like it often did when she lied.

"Why is he doing this? What does he care if my daughters die or are sold?"

"Birk is a caring man," she shot back.

"No one is that caring."

Lily couldn't say it was the Guardian's desire to eradicate all human trafficking from the realm because no one was to learn of their identity. "I think he's hoping that in the process of fighting, a few of Dorlack's men will die—including Dorlack himself."

"Assuming he even shows up."

Her stomach cramped. Had Birk thought about that possibility? Powerful men often sent their underlings to do the job. Crap.

Toma started the engine and pulled into the road. "I still don't like it. Caspian is up to something."

Let him think that.

The next few hours were going to be incredibly uncomfortable enough, but if she was cuffed like this, it would make it doubly so. "Can't you take these off me now? I'm not going to jump out of a moving car. If anyone is watching, won't it look a little funny that my left arm instead of my right is holding onto the handle above the door? Dorlack's dragon goons are probably flying overhead right now and will stay there until we reach Glen Meadow."

"Fuck. Okay, once we leave town, I'll uncuff you."

"Thank you." A stoplight turned red and Toma was forced to come to a halt.

He stuck one hand in his pocket, pulled out a key, and unlocked the cuff. "Okay, but don't try anything."

"I won't." Once free, her shoulder and back rejoiced, even though she'd only been in the twisted position a few minutes.

If she really had been captive, she would have considered jumping out. Lily wouldn't try that because one of Dorlack's men might sweep her up and fly her away.

When the light turned green, he floored it, snapping her head back. *Way to stay cool, Toma.* Lily had a bad feeling about this loose cannon.

WHEN BIRK SPOTTED Toma's truck pull into the gas station, he cloaked himself and made a beeline toward it. The plan was for Toma to gas up and then go to the rendezvous point. Simple—but easy to mess up.

To keep from being seen, Birk landed behind the station. For ease of stealth and mobility, he shifted back into his human form. As much as he wanted to rush out and hold Lily in his arms, he had to wait until she entered the small store attached to the gas station. Tory would take her place, and Toma would leave. Then and only then would Birk find his future mate.

On the side of the station, out of view of any surveillance cameras, sat Nessa's car. He eased over to it and tapped on the driver's seat window. Logan rolled it down. "Hey."

"Is Tory inside?" Birk asked.

"Yup. She's been waiting for Lily in there. After she arrives, Tory will wait a few minutes to make it look like a legit bathroom break, and then come out," Logan said.

Good. Even if Toma noticed Tory wasn't Lily, it hardly mattered. Sure, he'd be pissed, but it would give him more incentive to demand the release of his daughters first.

A whooshing sound overhead drew Birk's gaze upward. Two dark brown dragons were headed in the direction of the warehouse. Birk had seen a few of them with that coloring near the exchange point, implying they were probably Dorlack's men.

"I'm going to check to see if it's all clear," Birk said. "I'll make sure Lily is okay and then take off."

"Kill Dorlack for us," Logan said.

Birk smiled. "You can count on it."

From where Logan had parked, he didn't have a view of the pumps or the front of the little store, so Birk edged his way to the corner and quickly looked. Toma's truck was now parked in front of the store and not by the gas pumps. He must have finished gassing up and was now paying inside. More than likely, he wanted to make sure Lily hadn't escaped out the back.

A minute later, Toma exited with Tory right behind him. Because they were under an overhang, it would be difficult for any flying dragon to see them. If Toma planned it that way, Birk had to hand it to him. It was a smart move.

Tory slipped into the front seat, and a moment later, the truck took off.

Show time.

Given it would take Toma about seven minutes to drive to the warehouse, Birk would be able to make sure Lily was okay before he went into battle.

He ducked into the store and looked around but didn't see her. His heart raced, and he forced himself to at least appear outwardly calm. Lily must be hiding in the women's bathroom just as Tory had instructed, but that wasn't going to stop him.

He marched down the small corridor that led to the male and female bathrooms and knocked on the woman's door. "Lily? It's me, Birk."

Feet scraped, and a second later, the door opened. At the sight of her, his dragon shot heat to every pore as his body pulsed light.

She threw herself into his arms and pressed her face tight against his chest. "I didn't think I'd see you again."

He held her close with one arm while he stroked her hair with the other. Nothing elevated his mood more than holding his mate. "Don't be silly. Nothing is going to happen to me."

"It better not." She sniffled, leaned her head back, and looked up at him with watery eyes. "Kiss me?"

He hated she thought she had to ask. "Always."

When he pressed his lips to hers, his hands tightened their hold and his inner dragon shot fire up his spine. Teasing open her lips, he delved in. Big mistake. His cock hardened and his brain function stopped.

Only when Lily groaned, did Birk lean back. "I can't get started," he huffed out. "Or Dorlack might get away."

She stroked his face and looked up at him with her beautiful blue eyes. "Then go save the world. I love you!"

His heart swelled. The last time she said anything like that, she only *thought* she loved him. Birk kissed her quick. "I love you too, Lily." He stepped back and lightly swatted her butt. "Stay another five minutes and then leave. Nessa and Logan are parked right next to the building."

She smiled. "Tory told me. You don't think it's safe to leave now?"

He'd seen two dragons fly by, but there could be more. "Not yet. It might not even be safe for me to go out. Once I shift, I'll cloak quickly so they can't find me."

Lily hugged him once more. "Come back to me."

He kissed the top of her head. "I promise."

HAVING BIRK STOP by had lowered Lily's blood pressure tremendously, but now Tory was in the hot seat. All Lily had to do was walk out of the store, turn right, and slip into the backseat of Nessa's car. Easy.

After she waited five more minutes, she pushed open the bathroom door. Good. No one was there. As she turned to head down the short hallway, someone grabbed her from behind and pressed a cloth against her face.

What the hell? Adrenaline flooded her system. On pure flight instinct, Lily jabbed her elbow into her attacker's stomach and stomped on the instep. A grunt sounded, but the pressure didn't let up.

Then a burning stench clogged her throat and rendered her muscles immobile. Her eyes rolled back in her head as her knees buckled.

Chapter Twenty

KNOWING LILY WAS safe energized Birk. Remaining in his cloaked form, he raced over to the warehouse, ready to take on Dorlack and his men. The rest of the Guardians who had flown there were already circling in their cloaked form. Birk almost laughed thinking how surprised Dorlack would be when he thought Lily would step out of the truck, and instead Tory would transform into a dragon. Once that happened, it would be the Guardians' signal to charge in.

The whine of an engine sounded on the pavement as Toma's truck slowed. It was almost if he was waiting for a mass of people to attack and rip him out of the driver's seat. He was right to be cautious. The double cross could still happen.

As soon as Toma made it through the gate, three men stepped out from the warehouse, forcing him to stop in front of them. One of the men was Dorlack, and it took all of Birk's control not to swoop in and rip out the man's heart right then and there. Sure, it would be three against one and more to come, but this man was pure evil.

The driver's side door opened, and Toma stepped out. Thankfully, Tory remained in the truck. He and Dorlack exchanged words for a bit, but it was when Toma grabbed Dorlack's lapels that things became interesting.

Dorlack shoved him back. Birk bet that if Toma had been a dragon shifter, the two would be in the air right now battling it out. Dorlack held up his hands and then said something to one of his men. While Birk had never seen a panther shifter and a dragon shifter fight, he bet the cat could do some damage. Panthers were powerful animals.

Toma slowly returned to his truck, only this time he walked to the passenger side. Shit. Dorlack must have demanded he see Lily first—or rather Tory. Fire burned hot in Birk's gut.

Both of Dorlack's flunkies stepped back into the warehouse and returned a moment later with Toma's two daughters. Thankfully, they looked unharmed but very scared. Both were slightly unclean, but at least they were safe—or were almost safe. Birk hadn't expected Dorlack to come through on his promise. In a way, that almost pissed Birk off more. The man must want Lily badly to turn over the two women who were sure to provide him with a nice return.

Toma opened the door to his truck and Tory stepped out, head down and slightly slumped over, acting quite submissive.

Dorlack yelled, "Come over here."

Even at Birk's distance, he could hear the harsh command.

I'm ready, his dragon said, beating his wings faster and shooting more power into Birk's veins.

As Tory shuffled toward Dorlack, Toma's two daughters took off for their father's truck. Toma stepped backward as if he expected Dorlack to pull a gun and shoot him. Birk wouldn't be surprised if he did. Then the man would have Tory and the two daughters.

Dorlack grabbed Tory's arm and lifted her chin. "What the fuck?"

As he reached for his gun, Tory wrenched her arm out of his grasp and managed to step back a few feet before shifting.

Even though Birk couldn't see Dorlack's expression, he bet the man was quite surprised at that turn of events. Thanks to Magnolia, Tory didn't have a dragon shifter scent, so it would have stunned him when she shifted.

As if the Guardians had choreographed it in advance, six of them appeared just as Dorlack and his two men shifted into their dragon form.

The two daughters jumped in the backseat just as Toma revved up his engine and shot backward, spitting gravel in every direction. Dorlack probably wouldn't try to stop him only because he had other things on his mind—like staying alive.

Tory shot upward and was immediately met by another dark brown dragon who was uncloaked. Birk wasn't worried. Tory could handle herself quite well in battle.

Because he'd told his men that Dorlack was his, they agreed to help only if need be. With his target in his line of sight, Birk shot straight toward Dorlack's chest. Right before he reached him though, one of Dorlack's two lackeys shot between them, causing Birk to abort. Damn. Changing tactics, Birk dove underneath his adversary, ready to drive his claws upward into the dragon's chest. He'd almost reached the right altitude to make the transition when someone from behind crashed into his tail, and the impact threw him off course. Birk wavered. Fighting three at once sucked, but he would if it meant he'd have access to Dorlack.

A quick glance to the side let him know that each of the other six Guardians were busy taking care of their attackers. Guess it was three against one. Dorlack opened his mouth and shot fire at Birk almost as if to mock him.

Birk would show him. With the image of Lily firmly in his mind's eye, he charged again. This time he was ready for an intercept or two. Instead of traveling in a straight line, he deviated his flight at the last minute, and then swooped up and over Dorlack. Nose down, Birk dove at him. While that move wouldn't kill Dorlack, tearing a wing would injure him enough to hinder his ability to fly.

With his talons extended, Birk grabbed a hold of Dorlack's wing and tugged. A shriek blew out of Dorlack's mouth just as the top bone of his wing bent. Birk's victory was short lived however, when both of the man's minions attacked him, clawing at his back and wing.

Pain sliced through him, and his animal shrieked. Furious that he let those two goons temporarily best him, Birk had to incapacitate them before going after Dorlack. His main adversary wouldn't try anything for another minute while he recovered.

Birk flew toward the sun and waited for the two dragons to come after him. They did. As they soared toward him, Birk whipped his tail back and forth, building momentum. Just as they were within a few feet of him, he turned around and swung his tail at the men. The impact caused them to crash into each other, and they tumbled.

As they were righting themselves, Birk attacked. Claws out, he shot under one of Dorlack's men and then flipped him over, taking him by surprise. With a huge upward force, Birk stabbed his claws into the man's chest and dug hard. The dragon let out a roar before going limp.

One down, one to go. Then he'd kill Dorlack.

Birk released his hold just as the second dragon attacked. Before Birk could turn around, his attacker clawed Birk's wing, managing to dig a hole in it. Shit. A loud roar sounded below him. It came from Dorlack, who appeared to be calling off his man. What the fuck?

But hell, if Dorlack wanted a fight to the death, Birk was more than happy to oblige. The problem was that Birk's ability to maneuver was now hindered, but that wouldn't stop him. Dorlack needed to die, because Birk had to keep Lily safe.

With his claws out, and his wings pinned back, Dorlack charged and managed to grab hold of Birk's chest, and a searing ache shot through him. He'd been in this position before, but for the life of him, he couldn't remember what to do next.

Then Lily's laugh tumbled in his mind, and her sweet smiling face flashed before him. As if she'd given him some extra power, Birk reached up and clawed at Dorlack's eyes a split second before Birk chomped on his enemy's neck. While not fatal, Dorlack let go, giving Birk a moment to recover.

As Dorlack fluttered his injured wing, Birk sucked up what strength he had left and shot straight for Dorlack's heart. Birk's claw missed the spot on the first attack, but when he beat his wings hard enough to turn Dorlack over, he managed to stab the man once more, right where he intended.

Die, motherfucker. Die!

Fire shot from Dorlack's mouth just before his body went limp. Birk retracted his claws and let Dorlack sail downward to his death. The victory sent enough adrenaline into Birk's body to keep the pain at bay. All around him the battle continued, but because the Guardians seemed to have things under control, Birk drifted to the ground to mend.

Two more Guardians headed straight toward him from the direction of the gas station. It was Logan and Nessa. What the hell?

A wave of pain suddenly weakened him. While he didn't want to shift into his human form, he needed to ask them why they were there. They wouldn't have left Lily alone. They landed in front of them and shifted. He followed suit.

"What are you doing here?" he asked as they rushed up to him.

They both scanned his body and failed to keep the shock from their faces. "Are you okay?"

No. "I'll be fine. I just need a minute. Where's Lily?"

"That's why we came," Logan said. "She never showed. We waited as long as we dared."

"I rushed inside to find her, but she wasn't anywhere." Nessa glanced to the sky, probably checking for Kyle. The brief smile on her face told him that her mate was doing well.

"Lily sure as hell was there when I checked." Birk could barely contain himself. He hadn't sensed any dismay from her. "So where is she?"

They both shook their heads. "The back door to the store was open, so maybe Dorlack figured a double cross was possible and had someone there to kidnap Lily just in case," Nessa said.

"Once he had Lily, why fight me? On the other hand, I doubt more than a few seconds elapsed before we swooped in." Birk shook his head. "I don't think that's what happened. He was genuinely surprised to see Tory," Birk said.

"If not one of Dorlack's men, who took her?" Logan asked.

"Hell if I know. Right now that doesn't really matter." Blood rushed into Birk's head, blinding him. "I need to find her."

"Doesn't her ring have a tracking device in it?" Logan asked.

He hadn't been thinking clearly. "Hell yeah, it does." He patted his pants and extracted his phone. "Camden is tracking her. He implanted the GPS in her ring."

He called his brother. The phone rang and Birk paced, trying to ignore the fire in his shoulder muscles. "Hey, Birk. What's up?"

"Lily's in trouble. I need you to find her location." He put the phone on speaker.

His brother was smart enough not to waste time asking questions. "I'm already on it. She's on the move. I thought she was with Nessa and Logan heading back to town."

"No." He didn't have time to explain. "Where exactly is she?"

"On the road toward Edendale. Where are you?"

"I'm with Nessa and Logan at the warehouse in Glen Meadow. It's only a few miles from the gas station where the switch took place."

"Okay. She's about twenty miles from you, heading east."

Birk couldn't get a grip on anything. "If a dragon took her, I would think he'd be carrying her. If that were the case, they'd be farther than twenty miles away."

"From her speed, I'd say she's in a car," Camden said.

That made finding her easier. Maybe. "Thanks. Keep monitoring her. I'll touch base when I can."

"Sure thing," Camden said.

Birk pocketed his phone, happy that Nessa and Logan were with him. Until his dragon healed his wing completely, his ability to fly and fight was limited.

"Let's head back to the car," Birk said. "If Lily is in a vehicle, maybe Logan can fly overhead, and Nessa and I can follow behind. That way I can keep in contact with Camden."

"Good idea," Logan said.

The three of them shifted and took off. The flight was awkward and painful, but his dragon worked hard to heal him. A minute later they landed next to Nessa's car, and the three of them returned to their human form.

Birk withdrew his phone. "I'm calling Camden again."

HAMMERS OF ALL different sizes attacked Lily's body. Her eyes refused to open, and her muscles wouldn't move. Not only did her head pound, acid was eating a hole in her stomach.

Shit. What had happened to her? She remembered walking out of the ladies' room, and a second later someone must have come out of the men's room or something and pressed a cloth over her face. All Lily recalled was a sweet smell and then not being able to breathe or move.

Once more she attempted to open her eyes, but even that seemed to be too big of an effort for her body. Needles pricking her hands implied they were asleep. Her shoulders ached too. Oh, crap. That was because her hands were tied behind her back.

If Birk were here, he'd tell her to study her surroundings. She could do that.

Tires whined.

Large vibrations shook her.

Lily didn't need to be good at puzzles to know she was in a moving car. Unfortunately, her face was smashed against a dirty smelling seat. Ugh. Lily inhaled and worked hard not to cough. Right now, she wanted to figure out where she was without alerting her captors that she was awake.

As soon as she slowly eased her face away from the seat, a sweet and sour scent reached her. Okay, she had to open her eyes for more clues.

Wake up! she silently commanded her drowsy body.

The muscles in her right eye released, and she cracked it open. She was definitely in the backseat of a car. Rough blue fabric faced her.

"Turn here," a woman said, though it took Lily a moment to understand even those two words.

"I know where we're going." The man sounded disgruntled.

Needing to move before she cramped, Lily straightened her legs, only to find her feet hit something. Most likely it was the side of the car. Not only were her hands tied behind her back, her ankles were also restrained. Shit. Where was Birk when she needed him?

The ring! If she rubbed a finger over the stone's surface he'd know she was in trouble. After twisting her wrists, she managed to slide her pinky over the stone. Hopefully, Birk could sense her despair.

From the way the vehicle was bumping around, they weren't on a paved road. How long had she been out cold? If Birk were still battling Dorlack and his men, would he sense her pain and try to find her? Lily slumped as a wave of depression socked her.

Chapter Twenty-One

NESSA DROVE WHILE Birk stayed in constant contact with Camden. Suddenly, his chest was on fire and a strong ache stabbed him.

"What is it?" Nessa asked, looking over at Birk.

"It's Lily, thank god. She's alive but in pain."

"They just made a right turn," Camden said. "Don't worry. We'll reach her."

"What's down that road?" Birk asked.

"Just some houses," Camden said a moment later. "It doesn't appear to have any warehouses or businesses."

Nessa made a right turn onto a dirt road that appeared quite desolate. A few farms dotted the countryside, but no homes were in sight.

"The vehicle just stopped," Camden said, sounding quite excited.

"Do you have an address?"

"Yes. It's 12450 Haystack Road. It's the last house on the left. It's registered to a Phil Regales."

The name didn't sound familiar. "Thanks. We'll take our chances." Right now, Birk didn't care who owned the place. He needed to save Lily.

Birk disconnected and turned to Nessa. "Pull over. We need a plan."

Fifteen seconds later, Logan landed in his cloaked form, shifted, and jogged over to them. He hopped in the backseat. "What did you find out?"

Birk told him what Camden said. "I'm thinking we should scope out the place in our cloaked form. Moving around won't be easy, nor will looking in the bottom floor windows, but it can be done. After we find Lily, we'll shift back, and then break down the door. I might still be healing, but I can throw a pretty mean punch."

"And if they are dragon shifters?" Logan asked.

"They won't be shifting in the house."

"Good point," Logan said.

"How about you and Birk handle those inside, and I'll survey the outside from above?" Nessa said. "If I'm attacked, I'll be sure to let out a loud screech, and then you guys can help."

Both he and Logan smiled. Nessa had the best dragon yell of the group. "Works for me," Birk said. "Drive a little farther, but park about half mile from the end. We don't need them to know they have company."

With caution, his sister eased down the road. As much as Birk wanted her to floor it, she didn't need to create a plume of dust and attract attention. No telling what kind of surveillance cameras were around or at the house.

Several homes appeared as she rounded a bend, as did a small lake that was surrounded by trees. The last home on the left was on a rather desolate piece of land that was backed up to the wooded area.

Nessa parked on the side and all three exited. He turned to her. "Good luck."

"You too. I'll keep cloaked for as long as I can."

Birk hugged his sister. "Thank you."

With that, she shifted and took off, disappearing into the air. What Birk really needed was the ability to cloak himself in his human form or have infrared vision to see inside the house.

"Let's go," Birk said. "I'll take the right side, you take the left."

"Got it," Logan said.

"We'll search first and then shift to regroup. We can meet by the wooded area where we can hide in the forest."

"Perfect," Logan said. Most of the time, Logan was more focused on his computer work, but when he was on a mission, he took on a whole different persona—tough, detailed, and determined.

"I'll check to be sure the hood of their vehicle is still warm before we storm in, in case Camden's tracking device isn't accurate," Birk said.

Logan chuckled. "Won't they be surprised when we bust in?"

"I'm sure they will be."

"Do you really think fighting them inside is the best way to take them down though? There could be others in there," Logan said.

They'd trained in hand-to-hand combat as much as they had in fighting in their dragon form. "Considering my injured wing—yes."

Logan nodded. "Let's do this."

They both shifted and cloaked themselves. A few seconds later, Birk landed. A gray SUV sat in the drive radiating heat. Gotcha!

Even though Logan was invisible, Birk could sense his location. Logan headed left and Birk went right. The house was a two-story brick home with only a bit of landscaping in front and no large trees to speak of nearby.

Because his eye level was close to fifteen feet, Birk began checking the top floor since those windows were easiest to look in. As he moved from one window to another, one of his wings began to flicker. Crap. They'd never save Lily if those inside stormed out now. He wasn't ready for battle. One shifter he could handle, but multiple fighters? Probably not.

Concentrate, he demanded of his dragon. *This is for Lily.*

He couldn't afford to lose focus now.

One of the windows on the east side had the shades lowered. Could that be where they were holding her? If only they had mated, they could communicate. Birk promised himself the first chance he had, he'd rectify that.

Using his claw, he tried to lift the sash, but the window was locked. Even if he broke the glass, he couldn't crawl in when in his dragon form.

No guard was posted outside, and Birk didn't spot any surveillance cameras. All the same, he needed to remain invisible for a little longer. Once he'd checked all of the rooms on the top floor, he went to the back and checked them out too. He then bent down and returned the way he came, looking in each window.

When he reached the front again, his muscles tensed. There in the living room stood a man and a woman in deep conversation. Even through the walls, he sensed a dragon shifter, but he couldn't tell if one or both of them were.

One of the windows was slightly cracked, and he edged closer.

"What are you going to do with her?" the man asked.

The woman stabbed a hand through her short, black hair. "I'm going to find Kyle and tell him his sister has been kidnapped."

She knew Kyle? How?

"How are you going to explain that you know?"

"I'll tell him I found a woman by the side of the road. She was injured and begged me to help her." The woman paced. "I'll tell him that I took her to the hospital and then came out to the warehouse to find him. I'll say Lily gave me a good description of Kyle. When he comes with me, I'll kill him."

The man shook his head. "What about that bodyguard of hers?"

"Don't worry about him. When I attacked him on the roof, he had no idea I was even there. I put the rope ladder on the side so he would think I was some kind of demon. Trust me, he fell for it. Just you wait. It will be Kyle who will come rushing out to save his sister. That's when I'll cloak and attack him."

"I don't like it. Too much could go wrong. It would be a lot easier if you just kill Lily and leave her body on Kyle's doorstep."

She snapped her fingers. "Yes! After I saw Landry's dead body and didn't know who'd killed him, it drove me crazy. Fortunately, I was smart enough to watch Kyle's bitch sister."

"That'll drive Kyle mad trying to figure out who killed her." He laughed.

Holy shit! This was Landry Madison's sister, and she was out for revenge.

Birk needed to move fast. He soared up and over to the other side of the house. Finding his brother was easy, but they'd have to be in their human form in order to communicate. Birk drew near enough to show Logan he needed to head to the wooded area. As soon as he shifted, he'd be exposed, but that couldn't be helped.

Once in his human form, Birk darted into the woods and squatted behind a large tree.

Logan joined him a few seconds later. "Did you see anything?" Logan asked.

"Yes. They have Lily and plan to kill her. We have to go now!"

"What about Nessa? We need to tell her."

"There isn't time. She can handle herself. We need to get Lily out first."

Tension high, they both shifted back. A few seconds later, they landed in front of the house, and returned to their human form. Birk's swift kick nearly crushed the door, and it banged open. They were immediately met by two sets of wide eyes.

"You!" the woman said.

Birk felt no need to comment. The man whipped out a gun from behind his back and waved it at them. He must not be a dragon shifter or he'd know that a bullet would be painful but not deadly.

Regardless, Birk held up his hands. "Just came for what's mine."

"And what's that?" the tall brunette asked.

Like she didn't know. "The woman you kidnapped. Lily Harper. We tracked her here."

As if he'd said some trigger word, the woman turned and raced toward the back. He suspected she wanted to shift, hoping to stop them once they had Lily. Birk wasn't worried. Nessa would take care of her. Landry's sister might have been able to hide from him, but one of the Four Sisters had given both Nessa and Kyle the power to detect a person if they became invisible in their human form. It was how Kyle defeated this woman's brother.

The man's arm trembled as Logan approached him. "Put the gun down. We're trained mercenaries."

Birk almost laughed. He hadn't heard that claim before.

"Stay with him while I find Lily," Birk said. As he passed the man, the guy stepped back, swiveled, and fired at Logan. What the hell?

Birk spun around. Logan must have expected the move because he was on the ground a split second before the bullet reached him. Because Birk was standing next to the assailant, he did a roundhouse kick and knocked the gun from the man's hand, and the weapon skittered across the floor.

Logan scooted forward and grabbed the gun. He stood and pointed it at the human. "Don't move."

Stupid man. How had he been assigned to grab Lily? Maybe he was the woman's lover. A bullet would do some damage to him. "Tie him up or something," Birk said as he ran upstairs.

Not bothering to ask the ass where Lily was, he rushed to the room with the shades. The door was locked, but that wasn't going to stop Birk. With a quick shoulder shove, the crappy lock busted and the door swung open. Gagged and tied to the bed was his mate, and Birk had to tamp down his rage at seeing her like that. To think those assholes had their hands on her. He growled. She better not be harmed in any way, or he would definitely shoot that asshole downstairs.

Birk rushed over to Lily, her eyes wide with relief and fear. "Oh, baby. I'm here. Let me undo this gag."

The moment he slipped it off, she sucked in a breath and nearly choked. "You found me!"

Tears trickled down her cheeks, and he wiped them away. "I did. The ring led me to you."

"I'll never take it off."

"Good. Now let me see about getting you undone."

A rope was wrapped around her waist that was tied to the bed. That came undone easily. The plastic ties around her wrists and ankles required him to partially shift a hand into a claw. Extending the talon, he sliced them off. As soon as Lily was finally free, he gathered her in his arms and kissed her forehead, her nose, and then her lips.

Birk had to get her out of there. "Can you walk?"

"I think so." He helped her off the bed. Holding onto her, she took a few steps. "Some woman drugged me."

"I believe Nessa is taking care of her as we speak." He'd tell her who that woman was later.

Even though she said she could walk, Birk wrapped an arm around her waist for support. At the top of the stairs, he stopped. "You still have everything under control down there, Logan?" Birk called out.

"So far, so good."

With care, he and Lily made their way down the steps. "What should we do with this guy?" Logan asked once they reached the living room.

"Take him in. He'll be charged with kidnapping." Birk faced the man. "I hope you aren't afraid of heights."

Logan could deal with this guy. Most likely Nessa would want to fly home as well, as it would be faster, assuming she sustained no injuries.

A loud shriek sounded, but it didn't belong to his sister.

Lily looked up at him. "What was that?"

"I'll hazard a guess that it was Nessa doing some damage to the woman who took you."

"Good."

They stepped outside and walked down the steps. A loud thud sounded in front of them, and a dragon appeared on the ground. Nessa showed up a second later and shifted. She loomed over the downed animal and partially shifted her hand. She then placed a talon on the dragon's chest above the heart. "If you don't want to die, shift into your human form."

When the animal started to move, Nessa slightly punctured the soft shell of the dragon. A moment later, the woman appeared. "Why didn't you kill me?"

"I want to see you rot in jail."

The woman laughed. "I'll just disappear."

"That doesn't mean you can escape. But I don't think we'll have to worry about that problem either." She turned to Birk. "I'm going to take her to the Four Sisters, where I'm sure any one of them can remove all of her magical powers."

For the first time since he found out Lily had been taken, Birk smiled. "What a brilliant solution." He turned to the downed woman. "I'm sorry you lost your brother, but he attacked Lily's brother first."

Lily gasped. "That's Landry Madison's sister?"

The woman glanced over at Lily and then back at Birk. "He deserved it. Kyle should have been the one to die that day, not my brother."

Lily took a wobbly step toward her, but Birk stopped her before she could kick the downed woman. "Take her away, Nessa."

"My pleasure." She shifted and lifted her up. Even if she became invisible, she'd still be in Nessa's grasp.

"I can't believe it. This was all about revenge then?" Lily asked.

"Yes, and I never gave a thought she'd be involved in the kidnapping mostly because I didn't know Landry Madison even had a sister. I figured that Richard Dorlack had double-crossed Toma and somehow managed to nab you, but I was wrong."

Lily sucked in a breath. "What happened to Dorlack? Or more importantly, how are you?"

Birk dragged a hand down her face. "Dorlack is dead, and my dragon is still healing me." He wrapped an arm around her waist. "We can talk about what happened on the ride home. The car is about a half mile down the road. Walk or take a speed trip flying?"

A real smile captured her lips. "I'd love to fly."

Birk's heart sang. "Then fly it is."

He shifted and then gently lifted her up. Because of the short distance, he kept low to the ground. At the car, he set Lily down and returned to his human form.

She climbed into the passenger seat and dropped her head back, almost as if she couldn't believe she was safe. Birk piled into the car and looked over at her. From the way her coloring was improving, Lily would heal quickly. "You hungry?" he asked.

Lily rubbed her stomach. "No. I just want to go home and take a long, hot shower."

"We can do that."

Chapter Twenty-Two

IN A WAY, Lily was glad she and Birk would have four hours together, so they could talk. She needed to come to grips with what had happened. Birk had already assured her that Dorlack was dead, and that Toma's two daughters had been returned.

"What will happen to Toma?" she asked. "He burned down his warehouse to defraud our insurance company."

Birk nodded. "He'll be punished. We'll turn him over to the authorities and let them sort things out. I'm sure that he'll be spending quite a bit of time in jail."

"Good. He was a creep."

Birk laughed but quickly sobered. He reached out and squeezed her hand. "I'm sorry, Lily. I never meant for any of this to happen."

She twisted toward him, hating the guilt in his voice. "I know that. I still can't believe that Kyle's assistant had a sister. How did she find out about the switch?"

"She probably followed me to the gas station and then saw you slip out of Toma's car."

"Damn. If it hadn't been for this ring, you never would have found me."

He looked over at her. "I did, and that's all that mattered."

"How is Tory?"

Birk reached over while keeping an eye on the road. "When I left, everyone was having a one-on-one battle and winning, but more could have arrived after I left. We'll find out when we get back home. Just relax, and try to get some rest."

Lily almost chuckled. "I can't rest until I know everyone is okay.

Kyle was with the men fighting, wasn't he?"

"Yes."

"Then I'll rest after I know my brother is safe."

Because Birk was quiet, Lily watched the countryside speed by. An hour later, her stomach grumbled.

"I thought you said you weren't hungry."

She chuckled. "I guess I am."

They were passing through a small town that contained a few eating spots. "How does the Yawning Cow Diner sound?" Birk nodded to a cute café. The awning out front was white with big black spots.

She laughed. "I love the name. I think it's perfect."

Birk pulled in front. He cut the engine, came around to her side, and helped her out. Her legs were a little weak, but otherwise, she believed she would recover quickly. A good meal would do wonders for her.

Inside the diner, Birk picked a booth near the back where he faced the entrance, which suited her fine. After they ordered and their drinks were delivered, Birk chugged back a good portion of his lemonade and then set the glass down. "I've been thinking."

"I hope so."

He smiled briefly. "Lily, I hope you realize that you are my world. Everything I do is for you."

She reached across the table and stroked his hand. "That is the nicest thing anyone has ever said to me."

His eyes darkened. "I hear a *but* coming."

Her heart dropped to her stomach. "There is no but, Birk. I love you. And not just because you keep saving me."

He stroked a hand down his jaw. "Let me ask you. Would you be willing to spend the rest of your life with me?"

The heart that had securely lodged itself in her stomach beat wildly. "What are you saying? Are you asking me to marry you?" She didn't think shifters did that.

"I guess I am, though dragons don't do the walk down the aisle thing—at least not right off the bat. We mate first. But we can do a church wedding if you have your heart set on it."

Wow. Her head spun. It was what she hoped he'd say. "Why haven't we mated yet?"

Every time they were in bed, she expected him to bite her. His sisters and cousins had even given her the lowdown on what to expect.

He glanced to the side. "I didn't think you were ready."

Okay, that took her by surprise. "You didn't think I wanted you enough? Or what?"

He ran a finger around his collar and tugged. "No. I didn't think you were ready for my lifestyle. Now you've seen what I do. It's dangerous, and I know you would worry about me. Too much in fact."

That was lame. "You are in charge of security at the Sinclair and Caspian mines. Being down in that dark, smelly hole seems more dangerous to me. I love you, so of course I'd worry no matter what you did."

His grin came out wide. "For real?"

Birk did have his silly side. "Yes, for real dragon-boy. I mean dragon-man."

Birk laughed, and his eyes turned teal. "That's why I love you, Lily Harper. You have such a fresh view on things."

She sipped her tea. "Thank you."

"So, it's a yes, right? You want to mate with me."

She giggled; something she hadn't done in a long time. "It's a definite yes!" She leaned forward, not wanting anyone to overhear. "Do you think you can handle me being a big, tough dragon lady though?"

Ever since she saw how happy her brother was after mating with Nessa, she'd wanted that too. So what if she'd hated dragons before. That was in the past.

"Of course I can."

"Good, because I've always wanted to fly."

Birk leaned back in his seat. "Then fly you shall, my beautiful mate."

LILY COULD THINK of nothing else for the rest of the trip back to Edendale. Birk loved her. Not just loved her, but he wanted her as his mate. Strong, kind, protective Birk. She couldn't be happier.

No sooner had they entered his condo than his sister called. "Let me put you on speaker, okay?" he asked.

"I trust you had an uneventful drive home?" Nessa asked once both could hear.

Lily almost blurted that it was the most eventful drive home. She and Birk were going to be mates—in the real sense. Telling Nessa before it happened might jinx things though. "Very uneventful. Thanks."

"What happened to Landry's sister?" Birk asked.

"I delivered her to the pottery shop where Acacia and Poppy were more than happy to strip the evil woman of all her powers. She can no longer become invisible or hide her shifter signature. I then delivered her to Anderson. Our cousin has his hands full now."

"Good. Have you heard anything about what happened at the warehouse after I left?"

"Yes. I spoke with Kyle a while ago. He's at SinCas in a debriefing. Apparently, a few more of Dorlack's men showed up, but they were no match for our Guardians. Several managed to escape though. I dare say it probably will be a long time before they regroup. If they do, I hope it's not in our province."

Lily clapped. "No one was injured?"

"Nothing our dragons couldn't handle. According to Kyle, everyone has arrived back."

That was the best news she'd heard in days—other than the fact that Birk loved her and wanted to mate with her.

"One other thing," Nessa said. "I'm not sure which of the

Guardians called, but someone warned the Edendale police what had happened at the warehouse. Toma is now in custody, and his girls have been reunited with their loved ones."

Lily stepped over to Birk and hugged him. He cleared his throat. "Thanks for the update. Gotta go."

Nessa laughed. "Enjoy yourself, brother."

"I intend to." He pressed the disconnect button. A second later, Birk's lips were pressed against Lily's, and her whole body felt like she had shed every insecurity she'd ever had. This man loved her and wanted her—forever. As excited as she was to think about the future, she wanted to enjoy this moment more.

Not breaking the seal, Birk lifted her up and carried her into his bedroom. Her body vibrated with joy, and her head almost exploded with passionate need. Lily's new shifter friends had claimed that the bite didn't hurt, but she wasn't totally convinced.

Birk set her down gently on the bed. He then sat next to her, lifted her wrists, and then turned her arms each way. "Looks like you might have some bruising, but that's all. How do they feel?"

As much as she loved that Birk wanted to protect her, there was a time and place for it. Now was not the time. "Good enough to be kissed and loved hard. Come on. No more worrying—only loving. Okay?"

He chuckled. "Loving it is."

When he continued to look down at her, Lily growled, grabbed his face, and sat up. She kissed him softly at first but then was unable to keep from joining her tongue with his.

It was as if she'd pressed all of his hot buttons at once. Birk rolled onto his back and pulled her on top of him, never breaking contact. She brushed her palms against the short bristles on his face, as he slid his hands down to her butt and squeezed, inciting her lust and desire.

Needing more contact, she drew her knees inward and sat on his hard cock. She slid her body back and forth, eliciting groan after groan from Birk. Their tongues whipped back and forth, faster and faster until she was ready to combust. This time, it was Lily who came up for air first.

"I want you naked," she demanded.

She slipped to the side and undid his pants while he sat up and tossed off his shirt. His large chest and rippled muscles took her breath away. She didn't like the red battle streaks across his shoulder. "Do those hurt?"

"Nah. All the markings will be gone by tomorrow."

"Lift up, so I can take off these pants," she said.

Birk swatted her hands away. "I need to ditch the shoes first."

As she slipped off hers, he tossed off the rest of his clothes in a second. Even though she'd seen him naked many times and had made love to him before, she was still impressed with his size.

Lily reached out and grabbed his thick cock. She pumped her fist up and down a few times before he grabbed her wrist. "Turnabout is fair play, baby," he said.

Because she really wanted his hands on her more, she let go and lifted up on her knees. "Have at me."

Birk licked his lips. "You have no idea what you're doing to me."

"Tell me."

"My dragon is clawing my insides, wanting me to mate right away, but I want to take my time."

Her pussy was throbbing, and her nipples were aching for his touch. "I'm kind of on team dragon right now. You can have it slow next time."

Birk laughed, his eyes glistening with desire. He started at the bottom of her shirt and struggled with getting the tiny buttons through the holes. Halfway to the top, he grunted. "Fuck it. I'll buy you a new one."

In one quick tug, he ripped open her shirt, and the remaining buttons flew. That act of desperation caught her body on fire. Without a word, she unbuttoned her jeans and slid them and her panties over her hips. She then dropped onto her butt and lifted her legs. Birk grabbed the cuffs and tugged. A second later, she was naked from her waist down. All that remained was her bra.

Birk just stared. "You are so beautiful." The awe in his voice sent shivers straight to her nipples.

Lily didn't know what came over her, but she dipped a finger into her wet opening, swirled it around, and removed it.

When she waved it in front of him, Birk's eyes shimmered. He gently drew her hand to his lips, and when he sucked on her finger, bolts of electricity lit her up.

"Mmm," he said. "I love your taste."

"I'd like to taste you," she shot back.

"Be my guest, but you might get more than a mouthful if you stay there too long."

Lily grinned. "I'll take my chances."

She rose to her knees once more. Just as she grabbed hold of his hard shaft, Birk unhooked her bra, and Lily let the straps slip down her arms and off her hands. As she leaned over to take him into her mouth, Birk tweaked one nipple and then the other, causing the tips to peak into tiny pebbles of hardness.

Wanting to give him as much pleasure as he was giving her, she drew him deep into her mouth and swirled her tongue around and around while she pumped her fist. The harder she kept a hold on him, the more pressure he exerted on her nipples. It was as if they were totally connected, responding to each other's touch.

When he cupped both of her breasts in one hand, waves of delight caused her inner walls to tighten. It was too much, too exciting, and too overwhelming.

Lily sat up. "I need you now."

Birk huffed out a breath, grabbed a hold of her waist, and lifted her up. She straddled him, and when her wetness slipped across his cock, the friction caused more waves of delight to pummel her.

"Baby, please. I'm dying here," Birk grunted out.

With her breaths coming out fast, she slipped a hand between her legs, and lifted his cock. In one slick move, she slid the head straight into her opening. Holy shit. White hot need hammered her hard. Her climax threatened to descend right then and there, but Lily wanted to wait, wanted to be one with Birk.

She dropped back her head and gulped in air. "Oh, Birk, you feel so good."

"You should be me." He lifted her up enough to withdraw his cock.

With a slowness she couldn't believe, he edged his way back in, each inch stretching her wide. When he reached the end, he slid his hands up to her shoulders and lowered her body down to his chest.

"Kiss me," Birk whispered. "Show me you love me as much as I love you."

The challenge tightened her walls around him, and liquid lust spread across her body. She nibbled on his bottom lip and then pounced. As soon as he opened his mouth to greet her, all thoughts left her body other than loving her man the best she could.

Taking back the control, Birk kissed her hard while he slipped out of her and then drove right back in. His tight control thrilled her. It seemed as if Birk was working hard not to come, and that was the last thing she wanted or needed.

"Bite me," she demanded.

What happened next defied all description. His fangs extended, and then he exerted slight pressure on her neck. She might have tensed if he hadn't withdrawn his cock and eased in again just fast enough to take her to the brink.

As his teeth dug into her neck, he drove into her hard and furiously. Her vision blurred, and her lower body heated with molten desire. Lily lowered her lips to his neck and sucked, almost as if her body needed to totally connect with him.

Searing passion soared through her as her heart did a rapid tattoo. She then shattered with the biggest, most explosive orgasm in her life. A second later, Birk's hot cum pummeled her insides. She didn't know when he had withdrawn his fangs. The only thing that registered was the incredible feeling of him licking her neck in a slow, soothing manner. The women were right. It really didn't hurt.

When the rolling spasms slowed, she collapsed on top of him. Lily wasn't sure what to expect. Would little wings sprout? Would her face transform into a dragon? As a ton of questions bombarded her brain, her body gave out.

When she awoke, Birk was in the bathroom, running the water. He returned with a cloth and cleaned her up before sitting on the edge of the bed. "How do you feel?"

She smiled. "Wonderful."

Birk stroked her face. "You made me a very happy man, and my dragon an extremely happy animal."

She laughed then sobered. "I don't feel any different."

"You will. Your eyesight will sharpen, your hearing will become more acute, and of course, you'll be able to fly."

She sat up. "When?"

"Soon. You need to rest first. You've had a very rough day."

"What about you? You went into battle."

"I did, but I'm used to it. What do you say we shower and then snuggle? If you play your cards right, maybe we can have a repeat of our last shower experience together."

Oh, boy. Life with Birk was going to be so much fun. "I like that idea. Race ya!"

Chapter Twenty-Three

L ILY WAS NERVOUS. Intellectually, she understood that after she mated with Birk, she'd be able to turn into a dragon. But what if she was the first human to fail?

He'd taken her to a corner of the Caspian mine where no one could watch them just in case the worst happened. "Ready?" he asked.

"To turn into a dragon?"

"How about we start with partial shifting first? It comes in very handy, especially in confined spaces."

"Like when you cut off those plastic wrist ties?"

He smiled. "Yes. Let me show you what to do."

Birk lifted his arms, and right before her eyes, his hands transformed into claws, like she'd seen him do before. A second later, fire shot out of the ends.

She stepped close but not too near. "How did you do that?"

He smiled. "I imagined my talons growing, and they do. Try it."

Lily was highly skeptical, but she closed her eyes and lifted her arms, mimicking Birk's actions. With the image of his claws in her mind's eye, she concentrated on doing the same thing. Not only did she worry about succeeding, she was also concerned that if she succeeded, she might not be able to return her hands to human form. Before she could think about that dilemma, her skin stretched, and then her bones cracked. She jumped back and shook her hands, not liking the strange feeling of something exploding inside her.

While the discomfort wasn't too great, having her body change so quickly had her heart pounding.

"Open your eyes, Lily," Birk said with pride.

She did, and when she saw how distorted her arms were, she immediately hid them behind her back. "They're ugly."

He frowned. "What are you saying? Are you put off when you see me in my dragon form?"

Oh, shit. She hadn't meant that. "No. Only on me."

The lines around his eyes softened. "You'll get used to it." He stepped close and drew her arms to the front. "They are perfect." He ran a finger over the back of her hand—or rather her claw. "Look how special your scales are. They're seafoam green—so delicate, like you. It is now my favorite color."

He let go and she twisted her arm, letting the sunlight reflect off her body. The green scales were pretty. "I do like the color, though I was hoping I would get the same deep, ruby red color like yours."

Birk's lips quirked upward. "No one knows how that works. Now hold out your hands and imagine shooting fire out of the tips."

She aimed at a patch of grass away from Birk and pictured a little flame coming out of them. Only that didn't happen. Instead, a fireball a foot in diameter shot out and caught the grass in front of her on fire. "Oh, shit."

Birk laughed, and together they stamped it out. "Lily, you are going to be one powerful dragon."

"Me? I'm just a little bit of a girl."

Birk hugged her. "But you're my beautiful little bit." He leaned back. "Trust me. When you transform into your dragon, you will be as powerful as I am. Maybe not as skilled, but you'll have the potential. In your human form, yes, you'll still remain a lightweight."

She chuckled and punched his chest. "Then you better watch out."

The air seemed to leave his body, even though his eyes were glowing teal. "Watch out? Does that mean you plan to train to become a Guardian and fight beside me?"

"No," she shot back without thinking.

Birk held up his hands, and his eyes slowly lost their luster. She hadn't meant to disappoint him, but she hadn't had time to think before blurting out that one word.

"That's okay," he said, his voice softening.

"I mean, can I try being a dragon for a while before I decide?"

Without concentrating, her claws retracted and returned to their human form. Birk hugged her then kissed her quickly. "You can be or do anything you want."

Now she felt bad. "Okay, so tell me how to shift."

"The same way that you transformed your hands into claws. Mentally picture your whole body changing. Once it does, move what will become your wings up and down to simulate flying. At least that was what Nessa told your brother to do, and it seemed to work. We've been shifting for so long, I don't think about the mechanics."

"Okay, so once I'm a dragon, I just flap my wings, and I will be flying?"

"That's the idea, but it's a little more complicated than that. At first, you should stay low and remain parallel to the ground. I'll be right next to you to make sure you don't plummet."

"That's not very encouraging."

"Please don't worry. I won't let anything happen to you."

She smiled, encouraged by his confidence.

"Here goes then." She inhaled deeply and closed her eyes. Picturing a dragon, her hands changed first, then her toes stretched, and finally her hips widened. The process seemed to tear her apart, and while quite uncomfortable, it wasn't as painful as what Kyle claimed. Her face changed shape, and Lily was quite thankful she wasn't watching herself in a mirror. That would have totally freaked her out.

"Flap your wings," came a voice from inside her head—Birk's voice.

It took a moment to remember that he had told her they could now transmit their thoughts. How cool was that?

"Flapping," she sent back, almost giggling at the power.

A second later, her feet, or rather her claws left the ground. It was time to look. Holy hell. She was at least ten feet above the ground. Looking right and then left, she was shocked to see she was about the same size as Birk.

"I did it!"

"You sure did. You are incredible looking, Lily. I am so proud of you."

Had she been able to transform her mouth, she would have smiled. For a few seconds, she forgot she needed to continue flapping her wings or chance falling—at least until she learned how to glide on the currents.

Birk swooped in next to her and shot fire out of his mouth. Wanting to mimic his actions, she turned her head away from him and opened up, but nothing came out. *"It didn't work for me,"* she grumbled.

"Concentrate. Picture fire. After you do it a few times, it will come easily to you."

This dragon stuff took a lot of mental work. She imagined the heat, the intensity, and the different colors. Inhaling first, she then blew out a breath. Victory! A ten-foot long blast of fire shot out of her mouth. How cool was that? She was a real dragon.

"Oh, Lily, you are so powerful. We will definitely need to train you."

"I don't mind the training process, but I'm not really up for doing battle. I'll stick to my day job."

"That works."

While Birk sounded nonchalant, she could tell he wanted her by his side in all aspects of their life, but that just wasn't who she was— or was it?

"Follow me," Birk telepathed. *"I want to show you how to ride the currents."*

BY THE TIME Lily landed, her wings were weary. Flying took effort, more than she'd realized. Birk shifted back into his human form and for a moment, a streak of panic grabbed her. What if she couldn't change back?

"Just relax, Lily. Picture what you looked like this morning."

Birk's calming words were just what she needed. One second she was a dragon and the next she was human again. She looked down at her arms to make sure she wasn't covered in scales. Wait a minute—the bruises on her wrists were gone. She held up her arms. "How did I heal so fast?"

Birk smiled. "You're a full blooded dragon now. I bet everything on your body has healed. After all, if you're going to live for another five hundred or a thousand years, you need to be in tip top condition."

She was aware that dragons aged slower than humans, and that while Birk was one hundred and nine years old yet only looked thirty, she never thought she'd live that long. "Really?"

"Yes, really. Though which part surprises you? Living longer or being healed?"

"Both, I guess."

Birk moved close and slid a hand up her scarred back. "See? All gone."

Her heart dropped to her stomach. "What are you talking about?"

"The scars are all gone."

Her pulse raced so hard, she almost became dizzy. She reached behind her and touched her lower back. It was smooth. Elation weakened her legs. "How did that happen?"

"Your dragon is powerful, baby. She healed you."

"Did you know this would happen?" Why hadn't he told her?

He shrugged. "I couldn't be sure, and I didn't want to get your hopes up. Personally, I'm good either way. I love you for who you are, not for what you look like."

Only Birk would say and mean that, and it made her love him all the more. Lily wanted to dance. Not only could she fly and shoot fire, she was whole once more. For a split second, she wanted to find that asshole Nelor Dobbins and show him that his handiwork was gone.

THE NEXT FEW days were totally hectic. First, they flew back to the eternal flame, found Fay, and returned the amulet. Their fairy friend was thrilled everything went well.

Back in Edendale, Lily did double duty. During the day, she went to work, but at night, she and Birk would take to the skies. Not having to worry about being attacked was glorious. Even Birk was more relaxed than she'd ever seen him.

While he didn't bring up her fighting with the Guardians anymore, she sensed his small disappointment. As she gained more confidence in her abilities to fly, dive, and soar, a plan formed in her mind, but she wanted to learn as much as she could from Birk before she did anything about it.

"Show me how to dive to the ground and recover," she said.

"Are you sure?"

"Yes, I'm sure. One never knows if I'm out and about, some jerk might decide he wants to harm you by attacking me. I need to be able to defend myself."

Birk stroked her face. "It could be dangerous."

"You do it all the time," she said.

"I've had a few years to practice."

The man was infuriating but adorable. "Just show me, okay?"

"Fine. Watch while I do the maneuver. Take note of how fast I am moving, and then when at what point I pull up. You'll see that I lift my head and swish my tail to slow my descent."

She kissed his cheek and then stood back. "Good luck."

He grinned. "Funny girl."

Birk shifted and was in the air before she could blink. He rose higher and higher until he was a small speck in the sky. Turning, he came barreling toward her, and her pulse soared. She dragged her hands down her shirt, fearing he was just showing off and might crash. He came closer and closer to the ground.

"Pull up," she telepathed, trying not to let him hear the fear in her voice.

"Not yet." Birk's words came out tight and full of tension.

She swore he would crash, but twenty feet from the ground, he swung his tail back and forth, lifted his head, and stretched his wings wide. The wind from his maneuver nearly knocked her over as he leveled out and swooped upward again. Probably just to show her he had everything under control, he faced his snout to the sky, and when he came to a full stop, he let gravity take him down again. He must have built-in radar regarding his location, because two quick wing flaps later, he was hovering just above the ground. Birk then landed and shifted.

Lily ran into his arms. "Don't do that again to me."

He hugged her tight. "I was good. Remember, I've been practicing for a long time. One can improve a lot in a hundred years. Besides, Thane trained me and keeps us doing drills—like the one I just did."

She snuggled against his chest. "I think I need to take my time and not rush into anything."

He kissed her forehead. "I couldn't agree more. Say, I've worked up an appetite. How about we head back to the condo and see if we can scrounge up something to eat?"

"Just as long as I can be dessert."

Birk picked her up and spun her around. "No meal would be complete without you."

Chapter Twenty-Four

THANE GRABBED LILY from behind and tossed her on the padded mat. "Ouch," she called out.

"Come on, Lily. You're tougher than that."

She rubbed her butt. "I am, but it still stings." After a week of taking self-defense classes from Thane, she wondered if this had been a good idea. "Are you sure Birk has no idea we're doing this?"

His eyes widened. "I didn't tell him. I thought you wanted to surprise him for his birthday next week."

"I do. I don't want Birk to worry about me all the time. I want to show him I can handle myself."

Thane smiled then placed a hand on her shoulder. "It will be the best birthday present he'll get, but your claim has to be true. It's why I ride you so hard."

"I know, and I appreciate that you're treating me like everyone else." She'd spoken to Nessa and Greer about their training, and they both said Thane was the best.

"I normally don't like to give any of my trainees a big head, but you are doing a great job. Really. Newly formed dragons are stronger and often more agile than us old farts."

She laughed. "You are an amazing teacher and very strong for, as you say, an old fart."

He rubbed his chest with his knuckles. "Aw, shucks."

She punched him. "Okay, let's try that attack again. This time, I'm not going to let you take me down."

"That's what I like to hear."

Thane approached her with both arms extended. With great

concentration, she ducked below them, stepped on his foot, and then wiggled and twisted so much he couldn't grab a hold of her. She had yet to learn how to toss him to the ground but first things first. Turning to face him, she jabbed a palm into his chin while she pretended to gouge out his eyes.

Thane grabbed her wrists for real. "Excellent job. I think that's enough for today."

"No. I want to be able to throw you to the ground. You said you'd show me."

He studied her for a moment. "Okay. But then we call it quits."

She giggled. "Promise."

"Let's move over to the mat. If some guy comes at you, I want you to grab his right forearm with your left hand, like this." He took hold of her arm. "Then with your right hand, grab the back of his head." He demonstrated.

"That seems easy enough, but what's to prevent him from pushing me away? Both my hands are occupied. He could knee me or swing his hands upward to dislodge my arms."

He smiled. "Good question. It's why you need to move fast." One second, she was standing, and the next she was on the ground. Thane then helped her up.

Wow. That was faster than she could react. "I see. Can you break that down for me?"

"Sure. With your grip solidly on his arm and neck, wrap your right leg around the right side of his body, placing your calf where his knee is. As fast as you can, push him away, and he'll trip over your leg, just like I did to you. That's it." Thane showed her again in slow motion. It seemed simple enough. "Now you try it."

Thane could stop her from succeeding, but she suspected he would let her toss him to the mat. As quickly as she could, she executed the four moves in rapid succession. While she succeeded in tossing him to the ground, her leg became pinned underneath him. All she could do was laugh.

Thane chuckled. "I might have forgotten to mention that pushing the person's body where you want him to fall and then getting the hell out of the way is the key."

"Ah. The missing piece. Got it."

She tried several more times until she could execute the move quite well. On the last try, Lily truly believed she'd caught him off guard. She clapped and grinned.

"Excellent job. I think that does it for tonight," Thane said.

Seriously? "What about our flying lesson?"

He laughed. "You promised this was the last thing."

"For indoor training."

"You are a glutton for punishment."

"Birk's birthday is getting close. I really want to surprise him and show him what I have learned."

He smiled and shook his head. "Okay. What do you want to learn first?"

"How to use my tail better to tie up my attacker."

He raised a brow. "I thought you said you didn't want to fight?"

"I don't, but there might come a time when I don't have a choice."

Thane smiled. "I can see why Birk is so enthralled with you. Your can-do attitude is refreshing. Come on."

BIRK DIDN'T LIKE that Lily was working so many extra hours, but he wouldn't complain. She'd accused him of being too concerned about her already. When he asked about her work, she'd said she had a lot of claims to process, since she had taken off so many days during all that stuff with Toma. He'd thought about telling her that she didn't need to work at all if she didn't want to. He could easily support her, but he sensed that her working was important to her.

"You almost ready?" he telepathed.

Lily had been in the bedroom changing for over a half an hour. Sure, it was his birthday celebration, but they were only going to The

Wing's Bar.

"I'll be right there."

Now that they could mentally connect, it helped calm his nerves. At least he would know—if he asked—where she was at all times, and he could sense if she were ever in trouble.

The door opened, and as soon as Lily stepped into the living room, his cock took on a life of its own. He could only hope his zipper didn't leave a permanent mark on his dick. "Wow. You look stunning."

Lily was wearing a tight pair of black, shiny pants, and a bright pink top that clung to her perfect body. She turned around, and he admired the low-cut back. Ever since her dragon had healed her old scars, she'd been showing off her body more and more, and he couldn't be more pleased.

"You like?" she asked, spinning back around.

He laughed. "I more than like. If we don't leave right now, I'm going to tear off your clothes and make love to you once more."

She stepped toward him, swinging her hips back and forth. "Well, it is your birthday. You can have anything you want."

"With you occupying my mind, it's a good thing the Guardians aren't needed tonight to take down any evil beings, or I'd be killed for sure."

She dragged a finger down his chest. "I distract you that much?"

"You know you do." He lifted that finger and drew it deep into his mouth. Her blue eyes turned purple, and her scales shimmered on her chest. "Yum."

Lily withdrew her hand. "I would say we should skip going out, but your whole family is going to be at the bar."

"They are. Nessa told me that Mom even baked a cake."

"Is this birthday more special than others?"

He smiled. "We go big every ten years once when we turn 110, and then 120, 130 and so forth. Come on, we need to go."

"And this is one hundred and ten, right?"

He tapped her nose. "Yes, but don't rub it in. You'll be there someday."

Birk still couldn't believe how happy Lily made him. She slipped her arm in his and looked at him with what he called her adoring eyes. That made his body surge with endorphins and happiness.

Once they arrived at the bar and stepped inside, one of the cocktail waitresses motioned them to the back room where special events were often held.

"Are you excited?" Lily asked.

"I am. Even though I've had more birthday celebrations than I can remember, I have you with me this time, and that makes it more special."

She stood on her tiptoes and kissed his cheek. "You always say the best things."

He planned on doing that for the rest of their lives. As soon as they entered the room, he stopped in his tracks. In the past, his parents and maybe a few of his siblings showed up. Today, all his cousins were in attendance. Helium balloons covered the ceiling and streamers were taped to the wall. In the center was a huge cake with two plastic dragons on top. Someone had gone to the trouble of painting his ruby scales on one, and Lily's seafoam green ones on the other.

"This is incredible," he said.

His mom beamed. "Everyone helped. Now sit down so we can get this party started."

They all laughed. For the next fifteen minutes, he opened presents. His parents gave him a beautiful watch. From a few of his cousins, he received a gift certificate for his favorite gym, where he'd been taking classes for a while. The whole gift card thing was a concept the dragons brought back from Earth, and it was catching on fast in Tarradon.

After all the presents were doled out, Lily handed him a card. This would be the most special gift of all. He opened it and read the message. Twice. He glanced up at her and then over to Thane who was beaming.

"What does it say? Unless I don't want to know," his mom asked and then chuckled.

"No, it's fine. I'm just stunned. For the last two weeks, Lily has been coming home quite late. She said it was because she had to make up her case work, but it seems she has been deceiving me." He tossed her his best fake evil eye.

"I didn't want to ruin my surprise." She leaned over and kissed his cheek.

"I'm glad you didn't. I'll read what she wrote: To the most wonderful man I know. Ah...blah, blah, blah. Can't read that in public." His face heated for a second. "Birk, because you've spent so much time worrying about me and my safety, I asked Thane to teach me self-defense, both in my human and my dragon form. I can't wait to show you my new moves."

His heart hammered. Thane was grinning ear to ear. "Birk, she is amazing. Not only is she a fast learner, the girl can kick some major ass."

"I don't know what to say. That is the best present anyone could give me." He cupped the back of her head and kissed her. He didn't care that everyone was looking. Okay, he cared a little, especially when everyone started clapping in unison.

He broke the kiss. "Maybe later, you can show me some of your skills." Of course, he meant when both of them were naked.

She laughed. "Oh, I plan to."

The group returned to chatting amongst themselves a bit more, and then Lily pushed back her chair. "I need to use the restroom. Be right back." Birk stood to go with her, when she stopped him. "I'm good."

He had to trust her. "Ok, baby. Hurry back."

LILY WAS THRILLED that Birk was so happy with her present. He really seemed to understand what it had taken for her to step out of her shell and not only ask for help—but to ask for help in learning how to fight. When all was said and done, she had so much more confidence because of gaining those new skills. Hell, she should have taken some classes years ago.

To think she'd been so dead set against dragons at one time. Of course, she had Nelor to blame for that.

Take some responsibility, her dragon grunted.

Fine. I should have seen what a jerk the man was, but back then I was thrilled that someone seemed to care for me. Yes, I now know that I was a fool.

As she approached the door leading to the ladies' room, the men's door open, and her body vibrated. She was still getting used to the ability at telling the difference between a dragon shifter and other types of shifters. This one about to come through the door was a dragon.

When the man's head appeared, her muscles froze and her heart lodged in her throat. It was Nelor. Holy crap. What was he doing there? He was a wanted man.

Her initial instinct was to duck into the bathroom and hope he hadn't seen her, but then her dragon told her to face him. It was the only way to erase all of the bad memories—and guilt.

"Well, well, if it isn't Lily Harper."

She squared her shoulders. "I thought the police were looking for you."

He stepped closer, and her dragon pushed her talons out of her fingertips. She wasn't going to fight him. It didn't matter that she might be able to take him. After all, she was strong. And fast.

But at the first sign of stress, she knew who would come to her rescue, and Lily wanted to show Birk that she could handle this herself.

"I did leave, but I'm back. Don't worry about me. The cops are too stupid to catch me." He sniffed and then sneered. "I see you mated with a dragon? Was it that sad sack Caspian?"

She refused to comment.

"I never would have thought you'd mate with him. Poor guy has to look at your scarred back for the rest of his life."

"What are you talking about?" She loved the look of confusion on his face. Lily lifted her hair to the side and twisted partially around, keeping a close eye on him. "See?"

"Well, well. I see your dragon healed you, but you still deserved what you got."

His bitterness cut a hole in her gut, and something snapped. "Get out of here, Nelor."

"Say what? You're giving me orders now? That's a laugh."

A door banged open, and the music and voices from the bar finally registered in her brain. Birk must have sensed what was happening because his anger surged through her.

Without warning, Nelor lunged at her, and her instincts kicked in. In one swift move, she grabbed his neck and forearm while she wrapped her right leg behind his body. Probably because he had no idea what she was capable of, Nelor didn't fight back, or else he was just plain shocked that she wasn't backing away.

Just as Birk rushed down the hallway behind her, along with someone else, she shoved Nelor backward, and he tumbled on his ass. The satisfaction bolstered her ego.

"Let her do this," Thane called out. "She can handle him."

Birk growled, but he kept his distance. Nelor rose to his feet and spit on the floor. "You aren't worth it," he said.

As much as she wanted to laugh and ask if he thought he was, Nelor spun around and walked past her, Birk, and Thane, heading most likely toward the door. Being bested by a woman would be worse than death for Nelor, so she let him be.

"I'm going to kill the son of a bitch," Birk said.

Lily didn't need any more grief over Nelor Dobbins. She'd put him in his place. Something deep in her soul told her he'd never bother her again. "You can call the cops and let them deal with that asshole." He still needed to have a trial for what he did to her the last time.

She touched Birk's arm, and he spun around toward her. The lines around his face softened, and waves of desire radiated off him. Her heart filled with pride.

Birk stepped closer and cupped her face. "You're right. I have to say, seeing you toss that jerk to the ground was the best birthday present I could have ever received. You are amazing, Lily."

She smiled and then winked at Thane. "There are more smooth moves where those came from. Maybe I can practice on you?"

"Oh, baby. I can see this birthday is going to be one of my very favorites."

THE END

HIDDEN REALMS OF SILVER LAKE (Paranormal)

Awakened By Flames (book 1)

Seduced By Flames (book 2)

Kissed By Flames (book 3)

WERES & WITCHES OF SILVER LAKE

A Magical Shift (book 1) – FREE

Catching Her Bear (book 2)

A Surge of Magic (book 3)

The Bear's Forbidden Wolf (book 4)

Her Reluctant Bear (book 5)

Freeing His Tiger (book 6)

Protecting His Wolf (book 7)

Waking His Bear (book 8)

Melting Her Wolf's Heart (book 9)

Her Wolf's Guarded Heart (book 10)

PACK WARS (Paranormal)

Training Their Mate (book 1)

Claiming Their Mate (book 2)

Rescuing Their Virgin Mate (book 3)

Loving Their Vixen Mate (book 4)

Fighting For Their Mate (book 5)

Enticing Their Mate (book 6)

Complete Box Set (books 1–6)

MONTANA PROMISES (Full length contemporary)

Promises of Mercy (book 1)

Foundations For Three (book 2)

Montana Fire (book 3)

Hart To Hart (book 4)

Burning Seduction (book 5)

Montana Promises Complete Box Set (books 1–5)

ROCK HARD, MONTANA (contemporary novellas)

Montana Desire (book 1)

Awakening Passions (book 2)

PLEDGED TO PROTECT (contemporary romantic suspense)

Panic and Passion (book 1)

Danger and Desire (book 2)

Terror and Temptation (book 3)

Pledged To Protect Box Set (books 1–3)

HIDDEN HILLS SHIFTERS (Paranormal)

An Unexpected Diversion (book 1) – FREE

Bare Instincts (book 2)

Shifting Destinies (book 3)

Box Set (books 1–3)

Embracing Fate (book 4)

Promises Unbroken (book 5)

A NASH MYSTERY (Contemporary)

Sidearms and Silk (book 1)

Black Ops and Lingerie (book 2)

SOUTHERN SHIFTERS KINDLE WORLDS

Bear 'N Dirty

Author Bio

Want 3 FREE books? Sign up for my newsletter.

COPY AND PASTE INTO YOUR BROWSER:
smarturl.it/o4cz93?IQid=MLite

Check out my latest interview on You Tube:
youtube.com/watch?v=sQo5pyyVMDI

Not only do I love to read, write, and dream, I'm an extrovert. I enjoy being around people and am always trying to understand what makes them tick. Not only must my books have a happily ever after, I need characters I can relate to. My men are wonderful, dynamic, smart, strong, and the best lovers in the world (of course).

I believe I am the luckiest woman. I do what I love and I have a wonderful, supportive husband, who happens to be hot!

Fun facts about me

(1) I'm a math nerd who loves spreadsheets. Give me numbers and I'll find a pattern.
(2) I love photography, so I'll be posting pictures—especially of my Costa Rican adventure.
(3) I also like to exercise. Yes, I know I'm odd. Not only do I lift weights, I love to hike and walk on the beach (yes, it sounds like an ad for a date).

I love hearing from readers either on FB or via email (hint, hint).

Social Media Sites

Website:
www.velladay.com

FB:
facebook.com/vella.day.90

Twitter:
@velladay4

Gmail:
velladayauthor@gmail.com

Google:
plus.google.com/u/0/116041077486216602121/posts

Instagram:
@dayvella